Rough Paradise

Rough Paradise

Alec Butler

QUATTRO BOOKS

The publication of Rough Paradise has been generously supported by the Canada Council for the Arts and the Ontario Arts Council.

 Canada Council Conseil des arts for the Arts du Canada

 ONTARIO ARTS COUNCIL CONSEIL DES ARTS DE L'ONTARIO an Ontario government agency un organisme du gouvernement de l'Ontario

Author photo: Tania Anderson
Cover image: "Hidden" by Sara Cimino
Cover design: Sarah Beaudin
Editor: Luciano Iacobelli
Typography: Diane Mascherin

Library and Archives Canada Cataloguing in Publication

Butler, Alec, author
    Rough paradise / Alec Butler.

ISBN 978-1-927443-62-0 (pbk.)

    I. Title.

PS8553.U698R69 2014   C813'.54   C2014-902308-1

Published by Quattro Books Inc.
Toronto
info@quattrobooks.ca
www.quattrobooks.ca

Printed in Canada

I live on a beautiful, magical Island Paradise of beaches, mountains, rivers and pristine lakes. My neighbourhood at the foot of the Steel Plant is a wasteland in the middle of all this beauty. My street is lined with small, weathered tarpaper shacks, near the coke ovens. The washhouses lean up against falling down garages with oil-soaked dirt black floors which line the alley behind my house. On the other side of the alley is a chain-link fence so us kids won't play on the five railway track lines that serve the booming Steel Plant. Not only do I live on the "wrong side of the tracks," I live right beside them. The sound of trains shuttling back and forth over the train tracks was the lullaby that put me to sleep at night when I was growing up.

In the middle of the night the "furnace faces" at the Steel Plant are dumping the "slag" and the air smells of rotten eggs. The sulphur stench of brimstone invades my dreams. My street stinks like the Hell the nuns tell us we will end up in "for eternity" if we touch ourselves. I feel like

I already live there. People say this island is a paradise like the photos of sandy beaches in the tourist pamphlets. They don't know the whole story. Or even a piece of the story.

The view to the right of my cracked, dirty bedroom window is of the hulking, monstrous Steel Plant. On the left is a view of the underside of the arching, asphalt Overpass that leads to the Library and the "lunch bucket" city on the other side. The street where I live in the Pier crosses directly under the Overpass that divides the city from the Pier. But our patch of tarpaper shacks, tucked right under the shade of the Steel Plant, is separate even from the Pier. Everyone on the island calls this place Slagtown because we "slaggers" live here. Half of the small houses are abandoned, but they all still have washhouses in the back where the men wash off the dirt and sweat of the coke ovens and open-hearth furnaces at the Plant. The rest of the island outside of Slagtown and the "lunch bucket" city that surrounds the Hell that is the Steel Plant really is an island paradise of pristine lakes dotted with sailboats, wild mountain goats, beautiful beaches, and quaint colourful fishing villages tucked into scenic harbours on the ocean. But these places are for the tourists to enjoy when they come to spend the summer. The filthy Steel Plant is the engine that runs the "lunch bucket" city and this so-called island paradise the rest of the year.

My old man has pork-chop sideburns and an Elvis

haircut from the 1950s although it is the 70s now. Dad is a "furnace face" at the Steel Plant. He works the graveyard shift in the hot as Hades open-hearth furnaces where they cook and pour the orange-red liquid steel. My father rarely sees the sun but his face is tanned leather from the heat of the furnaces. It is also his job to oversee the dumping of the "slag" every couple of weeks, directing streams of toxic waste from the chemicals used to make steel into nearby tar ponds. It is a job he hates but he does it to put food on the table.

My father is old-fashioned; he refuses to move into the spanking-new housing project on the Hill, near where we go blueberry picking every summer. It was built a couple of years ago to house the neighbours who moved there to get away from the stench of these unpaved streets. Dad is proud to be a "slagger," proud that he never smokes "tailor-mades," what he calls cigarettes in a carton; he rolls his own. Dad turns his nose up whenever he is offered a cigarette made in a factory. He stores his tobacco in a leather pouch. I love burying my nose in that pouch, inhaling the aroma of tobacco and apple. Dad believes the cigarettes he rolls himself and smokes without a filter, and the plug tobacco he chews and spits out, protect him from the red smoke that billows out of the giant smoke stacks where he works. It takes Dad less than five minutes to walk to work. Another reason he wants to stay put. Moving to the new housing complex on the Hill is another thing my parents fight about, besides what to do about me.

My mother, like all the mothers on my street, never leaves laundry hanging out on the clothesline in the backyard on certain days, and in certain wind conditions, or the bleach-whitened bed sheets end up stained red from plumes of red smoke pouring out of the stacks. The taste of iron in the back of our throats never goes away in Slagtown. The smell of the leather, the rolling tobacco and the slice of apple Dad puts in the pouch to keep the tobacco moist is a balm to my senses. The smell makes me feel safe, reminds me that my old man is one of the good guys. Dad is a good guy when he isn't drinking too much beer and off his nut about the "queer stuff."

"You want Terry growing up to be a pervert? No better than a drug addict? A prostitute? Or a damn thief? Homosexuals going around calling themselves 'gay'. Men wearing dresses and rioting in the streets! I can't even get my own daughter to wear a dress! What's their secret? I wish they'd tell me! Terry is sick, Ma! It's up to us to fix her, straighten out our baby. We need to listen to The Doctor and send Terry to the Butterscotch Palace. The sooner, the better."

Upstairs in my room, as I listen at the heating grate that leads from my room to the kitchen, I can hear them talking about me. I can see them below me through the old, wrought iron grate. I hold my cat, Pussy, in my arms, trying to keep her, and myself, calm. When I was eleven, the Stonewall Riots in the news was the talk of the neighbourhood. My old man couldn't get over it. The audacity of the "gays" taking to the streets and rioting made him laugh when we watched it on the news. "Good for them," I remember my old man saying at the time. I can't understand why he is getting so upset about it now.

Once upon a time, my parents thought my naughty, "tomboy" ways cute. It's okay to be a "tomboy" because, to my parents, it means I am still a girl. When I insist I am a boy, they're ready to ship me off to the Butterscotch Palace! When I was a little kid I thought the Butterscotch Palace would be a fun place to go. How wrong I was. I feel sick to my stomach when my older cousins tell me it is the nickname of the mental hospital. It is located in the middle of cloverleaf-shaped traffic overpasses that lead off the Island. The huge castle the colour of butterscotch is the last building the tourists see when they leave the Island to drive back to the Mainland. The Butterscotch Palace is the last place anyone wants to go. In my 'hood, locking someone up in the Butterscotch Palace is the threat of last resort. When kids are really bad, parents tell them they will end up in the Butterscotch Palace if they don't behave. The first time I heard about the Butterscotch Palace was the first time I got caught hitchhiking across the Overpass.

"Here's your little Beatnik back," the cops quip as they hand me over to my worried mother. I figure "beatnik" refers to what my mother calls my "wanderlust." Ma threatens to tie me back to the clothesline even though I am eight years old, to keep me in the backyard, since, according to her, I can't even be trusted to stay in my own neighbourhood. Ma warns me, "You're going to end up in the 'Butterscotch Palace' if you don't smarten up."

"The Butterscotch Palace? That sounds like a fun place to go. Where's the Butterscotch Palace, Ma?"

"Never mind where the Butterscotch Palace is. Just don't hitchhike ever again, do you hear me?"

"What's a Beatnik, Ma?" I ask after the cops leave, as she washes eight-year-old me in the washhouse out back next to the garage. She will not answer that question, either. She checks me everywhere to see if I have been molested, even though nobody had a chance to pick me up before the cops got me. I beg her not to tie me to the clothesline again, vowing that I will be good and play only in my own neighbourhood from now on. It doesn't last. I break my promise by the time I am ten.

In my thirst for more books to read, I started hitchhiking at least once a week to the Library on the other side of the Overpass. Reading about the rest of the world, beyond this so-called Island Paradise, is my favourite hobby and my saviour.

My cousins are convinced I am going blind from reading so much. They tease me mercilessly now about everything I do that's weird to them, like reading. The pals who hung out with me since I was cut from the clothesline are turning against me. I tell them to stop bugging me to hang out in the park across the street, I don't want to help them shake down younger kids for money, and get older kids in Grade Twelve to buy them beer. I can't stand the taste or colour of beer; it is the taste of hopelessness. When my old man drinks beer, he gets pissed, and starts yelling at me. I don't like beer.

I am so alone. I cannot trust anyone. Everybody I have ever known believes I'm weird now. I miss Ma and Dad. Right now, they are under the spell of this fucking Doctor who wants to send me to the Butterscotch Palace for refusing to wear a dress. I wish they would snap out of it and come to their senses soon. The Doctor is doing things that are dirty, bad enough to be sent to Hell according to the nuns at school. The Doctor threatens to lock me up in the Butterscotch Palace "until I am 18" if I tell anyone about the "special treatments" that he admits he believes will "cure" me. The Doctor claims the obsession he has with my private parts is essential for my "treatment." The Doctor says I should just embrace my vagina and enjoy it. I don't even want a vagina to begin with. I want him to make my other organ bigger not smaller but he says it's deformed and needs to be fixed. Most of all, I want to run away from this so-called Doctor who wants to cut my dick off. I thought doctors were supposed to help people, not torture them. The Doctor insists I will really enjoy sex like other girls if only I will give up this crazy idea that I am a boy.

The Doctor is forcing his "treatment" on me but nobody believes me. The Doctor threatens to lock me up in the Butterscotch Palace if I won't submit. He wants to operate on my privates, and have me committed to the Butterscotch Palace until I learn how to apply makeup and wear a dress, like a girl. I keep telling Ma and Dad that The Doctor can't make me wear dresses like a girl, that I am a boy. Ma changed my diapers when I was a baby. She knows I have an organ that is too big for a girl. The Doctor says it is an "abnormal clitoris." He wants to shave it back down to "normal." I insist it is not a clit. It is a dick. The Doctor prescribes female hormones that I don't want to swallow. I pretend to take the pills, spit them out as soon as my mother's back is turned. I resist all the things girls my age are supposed to like. I try not to think too often about killing myself. Fantasize night and day about escaping this so-called Island Paradise; sticking my thumb out and hitching a ride to the Big Smoke, like many cousins before me, is all I can think about; it keeps me alive.

I spend many rough nights under my dead

grandmother's comforter, surrounded by books, finding out about the goddesses and gods in the encyclopedia. I write stories about saving damsels in distress. Fighting monsters while at the same time fearing I am one. I read about "monsters" because the Doctor called me a monster the first time he examined my genitals. Reading the copy of Mary Shelley's *Frankenstein* from the Library, I cry when the monster begs the Doctor for compassion because I can relate. Am I doomed to be alone and misunderstood for the rest of my life? Rejected by society? Is The Doctor right when he says I don't have what it takes to make a woman happy? Will no girl ever love me?

I am determined to find out about what goes on in the rest of the world and if people like me exist anywhere. If I stay here in this so-called Island Paradise I will not find love. My cousins are drifting away. We are not tight anymore. I am all on my own. And, what the fuck is going on with my body? I like that my beard is coming in thick, and my shoulders are getting broader by the week. My chest will not stop itching day and night. I am upset that these absurd mounds of flesh, "female primary sex characteristics" The Doctor calls "breasts" are sprouting on my chest! Luckily I found a blue, working man's shirt in the Sally Ann donation box behind the Library, so I can hide these "breasts" in plain sight. Dad hates me wearing a blue working shirt like the one he wears himself. Dad doesn't want me to be a "slagger" either. He tries to rip the shirt off me during a drunken wrestling match on the kitchen floor. I win the wrestling match, so I get to keep the shirt on. I wish my old man would show me how to shave, but not if he is making me do it to be more like a girl. I want him to show me like a man.

Before I hit puberty, getting molested and killed was my mother's greatest fear on my weekly hitchhiking trips to the Library. The cops kept picking me up and bringing me home. I tell the cops, just drop me off at the Library on the other side of the Overpass. My father is laid off again. Hitting the beer bottle again. I can't go home right now or he'll whale on me. My only friend is the Librarian, I am pretty sure he's "queer" too. He slipped me a copy of Edith Hamilton's *The Greek Myths* a few weeks ago, which is more knowledgeable than the encyclopedia, especially when it comes to finding out more about the myth of Tiresias. When I read about the double-sexed seer in the encyclopedia I found out that Tiresias is called "queer" too, that's twice in two different places, *The Greek Myths* and the encyclopedia. I want to find out more about this "queer" figure of myth who switches sex. The word "queer" is yelled at me in the hallways at school. The Doctor warns me about being "queer," often while he's giving me his special "treatment."

"Hey, what are you? A boy or girl?" This is the

question on everyone's lips all the time I am growing up, mostly because of the wrong name. It says Teresa on my birth certificate but, according to my mother, my father started all this confusion by calling me Terry before I was born. Terry, according to my mother, is a boy's name. I love this name because it's a boy's name. I intend to keep it. Apparently, this is a problem. The Doctor tells my parents to start calling me by my birth name, Teresa. Problem solved. I *really* hate him now. I hate being called Teresa all the time, all of a sudden. In my head, I switch it to Tiresias, because it sounds similar to Teresa and like the figure of myth. The one thing I really want is to change my name to Terence.

My parents named me after a Catholic female saint, Saint Teresa of Avila. I hate it. I want to change it, since boys named Terence are called Terry. My parents read the lives of the saints more than they read the Greek myths. Could my parents have known about the Greek myth? Could they have been on to something? If I change my name to Terence, they would have to call me Terry. I bet they named me after a saint to make sure I get into Heaven, where they believe they are going. All these demands that I change to be someone I am not. I am a freak of nature and my body is being transformed overnight because of this thing called "puberty." The Doctor never explains to me how it can be true that I am a girl when I feel like a boy. Kiss the girls and make them cry kind of boy. My old man says I'm as rough and tumble as his nephews, my cousins. Now both secondary schools in the Pier know I'm a stand-up-to-pee kind of boy. I've been peeing like a boy since I was toilet trained. Ma tried to get me to pee "like a girl" but I reverted to standing up whenever her back was turned. It just felt more natural. The girls I kissed at my old high school were impressed every time I snuck them into the boy's washroom and used the urinal in front of them. There will be no urinals at the Catholic girls' school. My special way of impressing the girls will be gone. I have to figure some other way to impress the girls now.

I will impress nobody wearing a dress, which Dad is yelling at me to do. Everybody will make fun of me. Putting on makeup sounds like torture. I will look more like a freak in a dress. Then people will really be confused. "Just let me dress how I feel." I want to wear jeans, not bell-bottom jeans though. Only girls wear bell-bottom jeans at my old school. Now, Ma never stops setting the neighbours and family straight, telling them I am her daughter Teresa. Now, I have to insist that our neighbours keep calling me Terry, despite my mother's protestations.

Before, this confusion I cause everywhere I go was a constant source of amusement between Ma, Dad and me. Now, it is a constant source of embarrassment. I tell Ma to stop correcting people; she goes overboard in her efforts.

Do both my parents think I am crazy to keep insisting I am a boy? It was never a big deal before, but now that puberty has hit, they want to "fix" me. And, they want pretty well everyone else in our neighbourhood to help! I feel like the whole world has gone crazy all of a sudden.

At twelve when I start to grow my beard, my mother starts taking me to doctors. This is the beginning of Hell, with a capital H. Since they took me to The Doctor a couple of months ago, sending me to the Butterscotch Palace is being seriously discussed in the kitchen more and more. I wish they would ask me what I want but it never comes up. The only time this Island is still paradise is when I see one of the most beautiful girls in the Pier. Even if we never speak to each other, just knowing she exists make me happy. I will miss her too when I leave, even though she barely knows I'm alive, or at least I don't think she does.

I'm in trouble now, kicked out of public school and being sent to the Catholic girls' school as punishment for kissing girls. Even this punishment and being named after a saint can't save me, though. I don't want to go to heaven. I just want to get back to Paradise. I believe it is a place here on earth. The Paradise that I get glimpses of in my dreams. When I could wrestle bareback with my buddies and nobody cared.

That night I hear my parents through the heating grate talking about sending me to the Butterscotch Palace.

I can hear everything from my room just above the kitchen. When I sit by the wrought iron heating grate that runs between the kitchen ceiling and my bedroom floor, I can hear my parents fighting all the time, mostly about what to do about me. Getting kicked out of school for kissing girls is worse than hitchhiking. I am shocked that I can be sent to the Butterscotch Palace for kissing girls, too.

I hold my frightened cat, Pussy, in my arms, trying to keep us both calm. Pussy jumps out of my arms, and scratches my forearm. Draws blood. Leaves red, angry scratches.

"We don't want our baby turning out like any of the women in your family either, now do we?" my old man says cryptically. What is he getting at? He knows something about the women in my mother's family?

As far as I knew my mother didn't have any family. My mother is an orphan. My grandmother died giving birth to my mom. It is a beginning I don't believe my mother will ever get over. There was never any mention of a father, my grandfather, on my mother's side. I thought I was my mother's only blood until this moment. I have always been one-of-a-kind as far as she is concerned. Not for the first time, I wonder: did my grandmother give birth out of wedlock? Is my father calling my mother's mother, my grandmother, a slut? What's even worse, is he calling my mother a bastard? That's really nasty. How many beers has Dad had?

"Don't you talk about my mother!" my mother explodes. Ma rarely raises her voice. Then she stage-whispers to my father, "My mother was not a slut! My mother was raped!"

Ma looks up at the wrought iron heating grate. I know she can see through to that part of my room, right above the rocking chair she rocks in, knitting an afghan. I move back so I won't be caught listening. I should be asleep. It is harder to hear them talking down in the kitchen from my bed, so they usually don't talk like this when they know I'm awake. This revelation blows my mind. My heart hurts for my mom. I always knew somewhere in the back of my mind that my mother is a bastard born of rape and that she is deeply ashamed of how she came into this world. Now this might explain why my mother never wants to let me out of her sight. That time in the washhouse, after the cops picked me up on the other side of the Overpass, she could not stop checking me over. If only she would check me over after coming back from seeing The Doctor but I am older than that now, no longer a child, and she doesn't bathe me anymore.

The Greek myth about a double-sexed blind seer called Tiresias in Volume 20 of the encyclopedia is the only evidence I can find that there must be other people like me. Even as a myth this double-sexed seer had to be based on someone who once lived. Ma buys a new volume at the grocery store every two weeks. Dad thinks it's a waste of two dollars. I am thirsty for knowledge, and this encyclopedia is my only source. The Library lies on the other side of the Overpass and I am forbidden from going. My old man doesn't want me go there because there are books at the Library he doesn't want me to read. He hit the roof when I brought home a book about Malcolm X.

A double-sexed seer changing sexes every seven years after whacking a couple of snakes with a staff is just part of the story of Tiresias. According to the 17th century artist's drawing of the seer in the encyclopedia, they look like a rambunctious beautiful boy prince with budding girl breasts not so discreetly exposed under their billowing tunic, charging forward with their staff held high like a sword or a cross. I have stared at this drawing for hours. It could be me!

After this fight in the kitchen below, my old man came up the rickety stairs to my bedroom. My room is small and A-shaped like a pup tent. When he comes into my room Dad's shoulders brush the sides. All he did was rip down the poster of Brando as Terry from *On the Waterfront* that one of my aunties pulled out of a movie magazine and gave me. I had taped it on the front of my bedroom door. Wrote my name, Terry, in big black letters with a marker across the bottom. That's why he tore it down. No one could call me Terry anymore. Period.

Everyone remarks on how much I look like Marlon Brando when he was young, pretty and pouty. There are tons of stories about Brando in the news right now. *Last Tango in Paris* and *The Godfather* just made cinematic history as a comeback for Brando, as box office hits. Brando is everywhere. This year when he sent a Native American woman to refuse his Best Actor Oscar, the shit really hit the fan. I admire him for turning down the Oscar as a protest against how Hollywood treats Native Americans, and the speech she made was right on. I felt angry with the people who booed her. Brando is not the young beauty of *On the Waterfront* anymore; he rarely shows his middle-aged face in public. When Brando declares he hates acting, the newspapers go crazy. He is my hero. The fact that he doesn't want to be my hero makes him my hero even more.

All the girls say I have Brando's full, sensual lips. I love kissing girls, and girls have been kissing me back, since the age of four. People are amused by the idea of Brando on film being sodomized by a young, virtually unknown actress. Everybody make jokes about butter. It's titillating until the film is banned here. Then it gets serious. A lot of people who want to see the film are pissed off about the censorship. There is lots of talk about all kinds of censorship because of the ban on *Last Tango in Paris*. I want to be able to read whatever I want to read, too. I want to read Malcolm X. I learn about what happened to a poem called "Howl" by a poet called Allen Ginsberg, and a book called *The Tropic of Cancer* by a writer called Henry Miller. I want to read this poem and this book now.

Reading is my salvation. Riding my dirt bike like a daredevil on the dunes is used as a last resort when I am feeling really frustrated. The price of gas is sky-high, so I only ride my dirt bike once a week, usually on Saturday. But this blustery fuck of a day is a Friday, my last week of freedom before I have to start going to Catholic girls' school to see if the nuns can straighten me out. I could not stand the idea of being forced to wear a plaid skirt and got in another fight with my old man. I am starting to realize there is no place for me on this island paradise. I race around the dunes with my soul on fire, burning for freedom. The sound of the surf of the Atlantic Ocean pounds my father's angry words out of my ears. "You wear that damn skirt on Monday or else!" The immense ultramarine blue of the ocean and the sky come together on the horizon and seal me in, like one of those glass snow globes you pick up and shake. The sky meeting water feels like a prison I can't escape. My old man is still mad, at me, not at the school for kicking me out, of course.

"What are you gonna do, Dad? Lock me up in the Butterscotch Palace?"

"By Jesus, that's just what your mother and I have in mind! The Butterscotch Palace might just be the best place for you! Off to the loony bin, till you come to your senses and start acting like my daughter!"

The first day I met Darla and spoke to her, I was trying to be as inconspicuous as possible. I was not having any luck lying low and I stuck out like a sore thumb wherever I went. I was trying to save a starving cat that was hanging out in the school parking lot. I watched Darla as she put on her red lipstick in the side-view mirror of a souped-up Duster. The older boys meowed obscenely at me, and called me "Pussy Boy."

"Look at what the freak is doing now," they jeered at me, half-drunk before first period. "It wants to be a boy so bad but it will only ever be a boy with a pussy, right? A Pussy Boy!" They all cracked up at the joke made at my expense.

Pussy is the beautiful calico cat I was trying to save that day. Pussy finally came out from under the cars that morning before first period. I was down on my hands and knees on the parking lot asphalt calling out "Here, pussy. Here, pussy" over and over. I was determined to save her. This is why they call me "Pussy Boy" wherever I go now. It was also the first time I spoke to Darla. It was the first time

Darla spoke to me.

"Give that poor, starving pussy some food," were Darla's first words to me.

Because of Darla, the starving cat finally let me feed her some of my tuna sandwich and pet her. I will never forget Pussy arching her back into my hand, purring as I looked up at Darla as she put away her lipstick. Now, Pussy lives with me, here in my room. Sleeps on my bed. Purrs and purrs for hours beside me while I'm reading and writing this. I love my pussycat. It will be impossible saying goodbye to her. The day I reach my limit and can't stand this so-called paradise anymore, I will find a way to take Pussy with me.

WHAT IMPRESSED ME about that first day was that Darla didn't make fun of my obsession with saving this beautiful calico cat in the school parking lot. She told the others, loud enough for me to hear, "You can tell a lot about a person by the way they treat animals."

I told her to stop hanging out with those losers. Those guys were "good old boys." They got their kicks killing animals, not saving them.

Pretending they had guns, they started "shooting" at the cat eating out of my hand, and then turned their "imaginary" guns on me.

My nerves were on edge. I wished I had a real gun, so I could kill them all.

Darla turned around and confronted them, "Cut it out, you boners."

"Fine. Take your Pussy Boy, and go fuck yourself. Might as well, whore."

"Yeah. That's all you'll ever be able to do with a sick freak like that: fuck yourself."

"Yeah. It's a eunuch isn't it? Or, something queer like that."

"Yeah well, I'm queer too. So you losers can go fuck yourselves, 'cause this 'whore' never will!"

I wanted to kiss Darla, get with her so bad. I know we are meant to be together. I ache to get to first, second and third base with her. Every boy in school wants to fuck Darla, not just me. This proves I am a boy, for fuck's sake! Of course Dad can see it! He just hates his kid being called a "queer" and "sick" all the time. He wants a normal kid, not me. I wish I could get my old man to see me as his son again. I wish he would show me how to take apart my dirt bike engine and put it back together again. Not ban me from the oil-soaked garage where I love hanging out. But he won't let me. The Doctor says I have to do girl things now. Girls don't hang out in garages. Girls don't take apart dirt bikes. Dad won't show me how a car engine works anymore. Or take me fishing with him. All because of the letter "F" on my birth certificate, a fact which cannot be changed.

"You have to start learning how to help Ma around the house, stay out of the garage! Start doing woman's work around here! And, stay off that damn dirt bike!"

So here I am standing on the edge of a cliff on the beach, revving my dirt bike engine, not knowing whether to stay or go. Sobbing into the rough wind off the Atlantic. I feel trapped between the ultramarine water and the vast blue sky. I don't really want to die! Salty air stings my wet cheeks. Wishing things would go back the way they were before my fall from grace, before puberty gave me budding breasts and a beard and I got caught in the boys' bathroom with girls. Go back to a time when I was the apple of my father's eye, not the stink in it.

My father yells at me for strutting around the neighbourhood bareback without a shirt, breast buds exposed. I love wrestling bareback with my buddies.

"Where's my daughter?" Dad cries, over and over, knowing full well God is not going to answer his pleas. Dad drinks because God never answers. God is to blame for everything.

"Fuck you, Dad!" I yell, as I run out the back door and jump on my dirt bike to escape his anger. Wearing a dress, and getting a boyfriend; to submit to The Doctor will kill me, so I might as well be dead.

Everyone wants the real me, the boy I know I really am, to just disappear. Now here on the edge of this cliff, I have doubts. There must be a better world out there, a place for people like me. What would dying accomplish? It would let them win! Crying into the wind, I realize I don't want to die. I howl, like a caged wolf.

"Hey! Brando! What's up? Is that you yelling and howling? Are you part wolf, too? Full moon tonight, but the moon isn't up yet. Are you OK?"

It's Darla! She is wearing very red lipstick, and I am in shock that she is right here on the beach below me, looking up, smoking a joint.

I probably look like a big baby with tears streaming down my cheeks. Filthy in my greasy dungarees and uniform-like working man's shirt that I hide in the washhouse out back until I go out.

I was expecting that I would be on my own. It is incredible that Darla is here right now. I don't know what to do or how to act. I am at a loss for words.

"Hot wheels you got there, Brando. This summer I'll have a bike too, my old man promised."

"I just came here to ride."

"So, ride. No one's stopping you!"

Darla is looking at me like she is looking right into my soul, deciding if I am worth talking to. I don't want to lose her interest. I should say something, and explain my mood.

"I just had another fight with my old man!"

"Yeah. I came out here to get away from my old man, too. Is that ok with you, Brando?"

"Oh. Yeah," I stutter, completely disarmed. She is just being honest. I am being a jerk right now. "You fight with your old man too?"

"Never mind that. What are you trying to do? Kill yourself? Are you planning to jump off this cliff on that dirt bike? That would be a really stupid thing to do. This cliff's not high enough to kill yourself. If you really want to kill yourself, you have to go to the other side of the Island. There's a cliff that's really high and drops straight down into the ocean. Don't go there without me, ok?"

"Why? Do you want to kill yourself too?"

"Maybe," nods Darla, as she takes a draw on the joint she is holding.

"Why would you want to kill yourself? You're the most beautiful girl in the Pier. Everyone loves you!"

"What makes you think that? I'm half-breed trash. My life sucks!"

"When the nuns call you names I'll stick up for you."

"Yeah, I hear they're my biggest fans. They might be sending me to the nuns too for hanging out in the parking lot with those losers. We all got caught drinking before first period last week. I hate my life."

"Yeah, to top it all off my old man won't stop yelling at me to put on a dress, start shaving and wear makeup or he'll lock me up in the Butterscotch Palace!"

"That sounds like hell, Brando. I'd jump too if I were you."

"Then, there's this Doctor at the Butterscotch Palace who wants to cut off my privates, because he says I'm a monster."

"Any doctor who works at the Butterscotch Palace is a pill-pushing quack. My mom gets sent to the Butterscotch Palace all the time, she comes out worse than when she went in. You look just like Brando when he was younger, has anyone ever told you that?"

"No, hardly ever, you're the first one." Darla smiles, she knows I'm flirting with her and she likes it. "It's Terry. My name is Terry," I tell her. My heart pounds in my itchy chest with excitement. I wish she would come closer. I smell marijuana in the salty air. I want to smoke some too. I have been smoking since I was ten. One of my older cousins deals for the Artemis Clan. That source dried up when I dumped my cousins for always trying to cop a feel of my breasts. Calling me "Teresa" when they know I hate it.

"*On the Waterfront*," Darla says, smiling and nodding. She really is talking to me, now my heart is pounding in my ears along with the surf pounding on the beach below us. "One of my favourite Brando films. His character's name was Terry Malloy. Is that who your parents named you after?"

"I wish," I say. "No, I was named after some saint."

"Who wasn't named after some saint around here? Well, except for me, I wasn't named after any saint."

"Who were you named after?"

"Nobody. Nanny, my grandmother named me. My parents weren't even talking to each other by the time I was born so they couldn't decide what to call me. I'm just trailer trash anyway, so Darla it is. Maybe someday I'll change it."

Darla quotes Brando's famous line from the film, "I coulda been a contender!" and then she laughs seductively.

EVERYONE KNOWS DARLA'S story, or they think they do. They call Darla, the only beauty in this wasteland, trailer trash, and the high school slut. I think she's the most interesting person on this whole Island Paradise. I want to be friends with Darla. Her old man owns a biker bar a couple of streets over from where I live in the Pier, that the locals call "Bucket of Blood." My old man hates this bar and is trying to get it shut down. The nuns who teach at the Catholic girls' high school call Darla a slut and a whore, right in class.

According to the nuns, girls like Darla are going to hell, with a capital H. They do not warn about how much trouble you can get into by kissing girls like Darla, though. I guess only the boys' Catholic school got warned about kissing girls like Darla.

"Do you want some of this?" Darla asked, offering the joint. "Are you old enough to smoke pot?" We are practically yelling at each other from this distance. I nod that I am "old enough," whatever that means, that I do, indeed, want a toke.

"Jump." Darla dares me. "Just jump, if you want to jump. Get it over with. Out of your system. Jumping off this cliff won't kill you, though. Come join me down here for a toke. I dare you."

"All right." I like the way she thinks. So, I turn the key and start the ignition. I rev the engine, and make a big show of it. Then I have an idea.

"Come up here!" I yell at Darla, "Jump with me!"

Darla beams. She moves backward on the beach towards the tide coming in, she takes a run at the cliff from the bottom and runs up in a flash. I realize it really is a puny cliff. The most damage jumping off it could cause is a sprained ankle, if we land wrong.

Suddenly she is beside me. Darla climbs onto the dirt bike, taking the seat in front of me! She pushes me back to the tiny bitch seat with her butt and takes over the handlebars as she looks back at me. Laughing at my surprise, she sticks the joint in my mouth. I have no choice but to put my hands on her hips to hold on. She is in charge. Darla revs the engine to get it bucking, she jumps on the clutch hard and we take off towards the edge of the cliff. The wheels leave the earth, and the blue sky swallows us. We are flying through the air front-wheel first, free as birds! Free spirits. Free at last.

It is exhilarating to be flying into the blue, instead of feeling imprisoned by it.

Too soon, we land with a bone-jarring thump on the beach. We land upright, but wobble in the soft sand, then fall over on the left side. We scramble from underneath the bike. Darla jumps up. I turn off the key in the ignition. The back wheel stops spinning, quits spitting an arc of sand up behind us.

Laughing, Darla is first up on her feet. "That was the best! We really flew!"

Darla reaches out her hand. We touch for the first time. Our hands stay connected; she does not want to let go of my hand, and I don't want to let go of hers. There is a joint between my lips, so I suck on it. I already feel stoned. In my mind I see the Michelangelo painting on the Sistine Chapel that I was mesmerized by the first time I saw a picture of it in the encyclopedia. God reaching out to touch Adam, except in my head Darla is God, and I am

Adam. How fucking cool is that.

With her other hand, Darla takes the joint out of my mouth to take a toke.

"So, how's your pussy?" Darla asks, taking a draw from the joint. She is definitely flirting back now. Or is she?

I don't know how to answer, what to say. She sure is forward, is my first impression; I like that. The stoner girl offers the stoner boy another toke. After taking a toke, I still can't think of anything to say. "The stray pussy cat you took home from the parking lot at school last month. Which pussy do you think I'm talking about?"

I take another puff and pass. She heard the losers in the parking lot call me a "pussy boy" and a "eunuch." Does she think I'm just a cat lover? "She only comes when I call her Pussy."

"That's what you called that beautiful calico? That's original." She laughs.

"What would you call her?"

"Cleopatra, something queenly. The Egyptians worshipped pussies."

"You were there when your buddies started calling me Pussy Boy in the parking lot that day, now everybody calls me Pussy Boy. I hated that high school. Now the nuns got a hold of me. Going to a girls' school is supposed to straighten me out."

"I'm sure you'll be a hit, they're all queer at the Catholic girls' school, I hear. They don't have any urinals, though, do they?"

"Are they all really queer? You heard about my pissing in the urinals?"

"Yeah. I've made out with a few of those Catholic girls."

"You have?" I am impressed, and chest-fallen. She kisses girls too, why would she ever want to kiss me?

"If I end up with the nuns for 'drinking before first period', we should hang out."

"You want to hang out now? Or, do we have to go to the same school to hang out?"

"Only if you tell me more about your pussy," Darla teases.

"You're making fun of me now, like your friend in the parking lot."

"They are not my friends, Terry. I am just bored stiff in this so-called Island Paradise. What a joke to have to live here."

"My thoughts exactly."

We are smoking together, flirting, and still holding hands. Things are looking up. I glance at the sky and realize how different it seems. When I am with her, I find myself imagining the sky as a canvas of infinite possibilities. I have been high many times, now I feel it just by being near her. I want to tell her all my secrets.

"I am really scared my old man is going to commit me to the Butterscotch Palace for sure if I don't start doing what he says. Maybe I should start wearing a dress. Or, run away. Or, jump off that cliff on the other side of the Island. They want me to do only girl things, be a girl! But I feel like a boy! Can't they get that?"

"If you feel like a boy, you're a boy. Doesn't matter if your father makes you wear a dress or if he makes you shave. It's how you feel inside that counts." Darla explains everything very logically to me. Our hands unclasp and she strokes my wet, fuzzy cheek, wipes away the tears with the sleeve of her fringed cowboy jacket. I feel calmed by her acceptance. Finally, someone believes I am more than a "tomboy." My mother tells The Doctor and the family that I'll grow out of it, but I know different. I am growing into me, which is as queer as it fucking gets.

"Here, I'll prove you're a boy." She moves close to me. She kisses me, right on the lips! First base! I quickly move past my surprise, close my eyes, and kiss her back. I taste the cherry-bomb flavour of her chapstick, excited by the incredible touch of her lips. She darts her tongue in between my lips and out again. I never had a girl do that before! I feel light-headed, like I am going to pass out. Next thing I know, Darla pushes me over into the sand, and she is on top of me.

"Come on. Pussy Boy, show me what kind of boy you are."

I quiver inside. For the first time the nickname sounds like a come-on. The most beautiful girl on the Island is coming onto me! Maybe this Island could be paradise after all.

Darla is from the Artemis Clan. They live together in a trailer park outside of town. Everyone calls them "half-breeds." The Artemis Clan live and work just beyond the reach of the law, and grow and sell all the marijuana on this Island Paradise. The cheap pot is probably the only good thing about living on this Island Paradise all year round. The Artemis Clan is being pressured by the government to abandon their trailer park right and all the land around it now. The Clan claims the land has been theirs since time immemorial. Long before the government laid claim to it. Stole it. Darla feels torn. She wants to fight with her family. But Darla has big dreams, too.

THE NEXT MONDAY, I get sent to the Catholic girls' school. I got kicked out for pissing in the urinals. The nuns call me wicked all the time; they genuflect whenever they pass me in the hallways. I am a monster to them, too.

Catholic girls' high school is hell for a heathen like me. The nuns take demerit points off every day I refuse to follow all their rules. The number one rule is I refuse to wear the plaid skirt that is part of the school uniform. I defiantly wear my blue dungarees instead. The plaid skirt-wearing "queer" girls cheer me on, much to the consternation of the nuns. Shaming me publicly in the classroom is backfiring. It only encourages others to blaspheme. According to the nuns, all us "queers" are going to burn in Hell along with whores like Darla.

In Religious Studies class I tell one of the nuns, "According to your teachings, if Jesus came back today he would be excommunicated. Wasn't Mary Magdalene the whore who loved Jesus? Didn't Jesus love her back? It's all there in the Bible." I got the ruler across my hands for that; fifteen whacks on each palm. Corporal punishment. A term read over in the encyclopedia.

I write in my bed at night under my grandmother's quilt comforter with a flashlight, creating a safe haven, a cave. I hide this notebook under a floorboard in my closet every day, afraid of it being found. I have to write more than ever. I feel more alone than ever. The Doctor is ready to ratchet up my "treatment." The Doctor is really pressuring my parents to commit me to the Butterscotch Palace "before it's too late."

It turns out that Darla is sent to the nuns after getting expelled from the public high school for drinking on school property and general delinquency. We are the "heathens" of the Catholic girls' school together now.

In the locker-lined hallways at school we make out in front of everyone; we don't care who knows. We want the nuns to catch us at it. Others girls call us "lezzies," admiring us, jealous. I don't know what a "lezzy" is. The word confuses me. Darla tells me to look up "Sappho" in the encyclopedia. The Island of Lesbos sounds fantastic, but is that where I belong? Darla does; she really loves the girls. It makes me sad because I can imagine Darla thriving in this Sapphic Paradise, but not me. I'll never look good in a toga. All I know is I am in love with an Amazon who has the last name of one of my favourite goddesses, Artemis. I can't stop thinking about kissing Darla's red lips. Her endearments make my heart skip a beat. The way she uses her tongue when we kiss makes my loins ache with lust.

Darla tells me that, according to the ancestors, I am sacred. She heard this from her Métis grandmother "Nanny" Artemis. Nanny is the only sensible one in the whole Artemis Clan, the only one Darla trusts in her family to tell about our love. Everyone in her family is against our seeing each other, except for Nanny. I am too much of a distraction; I am giving Darla a bad name! Nanny is convinced that I am "berdache," an Indian name for people who were born like me: both male and female.

"Back in the day, people like you were shamans, teachers and healers."

Darla is blowing my mind with her words.

"There's a Greek myth about this queer prophet who is both male and female called Tiresias." I tell Darla excitedly how the seer carries a staff, and the part about the snakes.

"Berdache were shamans too," Darla reveals. "You read the Greek myths? I don't; too many stories about incest and rape. I like my grandmother's stories, about animals, they are like our myths."

"Has she told you any stories about snakes?"

"Snake medicine is healing medicine. You must have noticed the symbol for doctor? Two snakes wrapped around a staff. Shamans carry a staff, too. Healers have to know how to handle snakes, take the deadly poison and turn it into medicine."

The Doctor, who is no healer, tells me his diagnosis for me is called "Gender Identity Disorder." This disorder is the reason for my problems with puberty. It sounds like he got this diagnosis out of a medical magazine last week. He probably did.

The Doctor wants to commit me to the Butterscotch Palace. He is horrified when I tell him I have a "girlfriend." He wants to break us up. I think he just wants to have me all to himself now. He argues with me about the dangers of lesbianism. I insist there's no danger of me becoming a lesbian because I am becoming a man. The Doctor insists I will become a lesbian if I don't follow his treatment protocols. The Doctor insists I will never be a "man" but I am in danger of becoming a "mannish" woman and therefore a lesbian. The Doctor "examines" me in his office. Our appointments have been changed to his office at the Butterscotch Palace. The Doctor graduates from using instruments of torture like he used to, to using his fingers. The Doctor tells me the orgasms I have against my will when he rapes me are proof I am born to be a woman. That I can be happily married one day to a man, like my parents are hoping.

I want to die every time the rapes happen, but I can't stop them from happening. I am so ashamed. I wish I were dead. I want to tell everyone what he does to me on that hated exam table. The stirrups attached to end of the exam table are equipped with straps to hold my ankles in place. I am here at the dreaded Butterscotch Palace on an outpatient basis to keep my parents happy. According to The Doctor, "Aversion Therapy" is the treatment for "Gender Identity Disorder" and I have to say I am very averse to this therapy which I found out is mostly used on rapists and "queers." Now they are using it on kids like me.

WHEN WE MET that day on the beach, one of the first things Darla asked me was if I am half Native American. I said I don't know, I don't think so. But, it's so obvious,

I realize now. Darla is cinnamon-hued, like my mother. Like my mother, she is a beautiful dark-eyed looker, with a beauty mark above her full French lips. I love her thick-lashed, almond-shaped hazel eyes. That is where they differ. My mother's eyes are dark brown pools touched by sorrow. Darla, like my mother, has her secrets. I try to discover them when we are together. Crazy in love, I want to know everything she feels. I want to know so I can make her dreams come true.

Darla is the first girl I ever really fuck. Other girls at the public high school who think I'm a boy freak out when they put their hands between my legs. I have a pussy too. They didn't want to be called a "lezzy" like they call Darla a "lezzy" in the hallways at our former school. The way Darla calls me "Pussy Boy" makes me swallow hard. Makes my loins tingle. She calls me a "good pussy boy" when I grind her up against the buttress that holds up the Overpass. On her break from the biker bar where she works, she smokes us up and pulls me into her, her legs parted slightly, kissing me with those slick, red lips of hers. We kiss until there is no lipstick left; I love kissing her soft, naked lips. The hum of motor engines and the whish of rubber tires on the Overpass above us fill the air. I kiss and grind her. I want to fuck her more than anything. I have a natural bulge in the crotch of my dungarees, but since the last girl that freaked out on me I use a rolled-up pair of Dad's thick working man's socks to fill out the bulge after school.

"We are birds of a feather, you and me," Darla tells me. "So, no matter what happens. What you hear. We are birds of a feather." I pause to look into her eyes. Stirred by her words of warning, I stop massaging her "camel-toe." "Oh, don't stop. It feels sooo good."

"What do you think is going to happen?"

"If we can't see each other, for whatever reason. Keep your hand right there."

"Don't say that. Why would we not be able to see each other?"

"Well, you are younger, two grades below me. Someone is going to notice our age difference."

"They can't keep us apart because of that. I'll be fifteen soon."

"I hope not. But we're just a couple of queers. Remember, everyone hates the queers. You told me The Doctor is just waiting for an excuse to lock you up in the Butterscotch Palace. The cops are just itching to throw me and half my cousins in juvenile hall."

'We'll run away to the Big Smoke, if they try to keep us apart."

"Right now, all I want you to think about is touching my pussy, Pussy Boy."

"If the nuns could read my mind while they're going on and on about how we're gonna be punished and how I could go straight to Hell; all I can think about is touching your pussy."

"You and me, both. I think about your "mangina" all the time, Pussy Boy."

I almost choke on the smoke I inhaled when I puffed on the joint we are sharing. I ask myself in my head, "Where did this goddess come from? I can't believe she exists!" I ask Darla, "What did you call it? My 'mangina'? That's fucking brilliant!"

"I think about your 'mangina' a lot," Darla confesses.

I am in shock, thrilled and scared at the same time. "Really?"

"Come on, Pussy Boy. You can't tell me you haven't noticed. I offered to die in a hail of bullets for you in the parking lot a couple of months ago, remember? They might have been imaginary bullets, but bullets all the same. Before we really even met. When those losers pretended to shoot you."

"No one has ever stuck up for me before. You're my 'hera', Darla. That's what the Greeks call a woman who saves the day, and my 'champion'. See, even in the encyclopedia there's a difference between a woman who saves the day and a man who saves the day. Why is that?"

"Never mind all that right now, Pussy Boy," she says in my ear with a throaty, knowing laugh. "Show me your 'mangina' and I'll let you touch my pussy."

"You first, let me touch your pussy first." I want to touch her pussy more than anything.

"Just thinking about you makes my pussy wet, Pussy Boy. Makes me feel like a bitch in heat." I love how she talks dirty to me. Her words taboo, her voice music to my ears.

"Just thinking about touching your pussy makes my dick hard." I contribute, proud of my dirty talk.

"Touch me right now." Darla undoes her belt, pushes her hipsters down past her hips. I gasp with happiness as I realize that she is really going to let me touch her, finally, after weeks of making out. My small dick is hard but not big enough. I wish my dick were bigger. Darla grabs my finger and places it on her labia. I don't know why, but I hold back. I want to savour this moment. My finger disappears between the fold of her lips, where it is very wet. "Fuck me," she pants in my ear; I slide my fuck finger inside her. As easily as that I am inside her for the first time! Her pussy pulls my finger deep inside her. I'm intoxicated by her pussy scent. Her pussy is so hot, so wet and so incredibly soft. Darla's eyes roll up inside her half-closed eyelids. She purrs like a cat in heat. "More fingers please," she growls in my ear, biting my earlobe lightly. I bury two fingers inside her. She starts rocking against my hand. I start finger-fucking her. The walls of her pussy pulse around my two fingers. She moans in my ear and spreads her thighs wider. I plunge my fingers into her. Dipping my fingers deep into her, my thumb cocked like a gun, strokes her clit. She cries out, "Oh fuck, oh fuck, oh fuuuuck!" I love fucking the silken walls of her pussy, steady and firm, in control, as she writhes on the end of my arm. Amazed when she comes, squeezing my fingers inside her, over and over. My hand is soaked with her juices. It smells like strawberries. She wants to touch me back. Darla reaches out to touch my throbbing crotch. She squeezes my bulge; she licks her lips and starts to undo my dungarees. I push her hand away.

"Trust me," she says, her voice husky with passion. She brings her hand back. Her fingers try to undo the buttons of my dungarees again. I try not to panic. Darla tries to look into my eyes. I turn away ashamed.

"I want to touch you too, Terry. You promised, remember."

"I'm sorry." I tell her. She takes my apology for permission, and reaches again for my crotch. We kiss while her hand does what it wants. I am trying really hard not to panic, but I do. The fucking Doctor's voice comes into my head. I feel like my head is going to explode. I pull away from Darla's hand; she pulls her hand out of my briefs. She could touch what she calls my 'mangina', but she doesn't. Still, I can't calm down. "You really don't want to be touched do you, Terry? It must be really hard for you to let anyone touch you. I wasn't thinking, I'm sorry."

"It's okay," I manage to blurt out.

"No, it isn't. I read the signals wrong. All the other boys are dogs in a junkyard, compared to you; they beg me to touch them. I'm just not used to being with a Pussy Boy."

"You're right, I'm not like other boys. Does it bother you? I just want to make you happy."

"Nobody's ever wanted to make me happy before."

"Someday we'll leave this so-called Paradise behind, we'll find the real thing."

"You are so fucking innocent Terry, and so handsome, like a fucking prince in a fairy tale, or something," Darla declares, and kisses me. Her mouth devours mine. Our lips are so swollen already from kissing each other into bliss. She shoves her tongue deep into my mouth. I suck on her tongue. She probes the far reaches of my mouth provocatively then lets me do the same, like two baby birds feeding each other. I am out of my mind with lust. Darla pins me down, rides my "manhood." Looking at me the whole time, right into my eyes, holding my gaze, her eyes drinking me in, demanding I pay attention to this moment. Never forget this moment of her triumph. I never will.

"Who has the pussy power now, Pussy Boy?" Darla teases.

My crotch flash-floods and throbs. Darla pulls me

over on top of her. I grind her for all I'm worth, turned on by Darla's desire. Her moans and cries make me grind my hard little dick into her harder and deeper. I wish I could shoot cum inside her, make a baby with her. She pulls my dungarees down past my boyish hips. We are finally touching skin-to-skin, pelvis-to-pelvis, all hot and slippery and swollen, our juices mingling, and my dick riding her! Bucking my hips, thrusting my magic spear into Darla, I shoot my load. We both collapse.

The doctor is trying a new tactic to separate Darla and me. Darla's old man is the topic of conversation at the next appointment. He asks me what is I think is going to happen when her father, who is a former biker too, who thinks of Darla as his property, what do I think he's going to do when he finds out about us? Darla's old man is a very bad man who owns a biker bar and everybody knows it. Nothing her old man could do to Darla is left to the imagination. The Doctor explains that this is why Darla's mother is in and out of the Butterscotch Palace on a regular basis. Darla's mother can't live with the guilt. The Doctor explains that early incest with her father is why Darla is a lesbian and a whore. It is very sad and tragic but is too late to save her. Her father has ruined her for normal life but I can still be saved. This is why I must never see Darla again. He won't commit me to the Butterscotch Palace as an in-patient if I promise to never see Darla again. Darla is not good for me, the Doctor explains. She encourages my delusions and that can't be good; she is recruiting me for her own sick reasons.

"I feel it's in your best interest, Teresa. I wish I was told about this 'relationship' sooner by the Sisters at your school, I wish I could have warned you before you got caught up in this girl's sick games. She doesn't love you, Teresa! She is just using you for sex. She can't help herself, but you can. You can be the one strong enough to end this unhealthy relationship." The Doctor is determined to break us up.

Shock and anger grip my chest. I cannot speak. Now I know what everybody else knows, that Darla's father rapes her too, like The Doctor rapes me. I cannot believe the unspeakable has been said. I want to smash his smug face, but doing that will get me committed for sure. I get a grip on myself and tell him I could tell my parents about his special treatments. The Doctor changes the subject; now he goes on about my abnormal clitoris, and what are we going to do about that?

I want to tell The Doctor how I "knocked up" Darla with my "abnormal clitoris" the last time we were together under the Overpass, on the ground with the gravel grinding under us as we fucked, but I don't want to get either of us into more trouble. He might make me a permanent patient at the Butterscotch Palace for sharing such a fantasy about Darla. How did Darla know this pressure to stay away from each other would start happening now? Birds of a feather stick together.

All the stuff Darla told me about the Native healers from back in the day, and what I found out about Tiresias, in the same volume of the encyclopedia, is giving me hope. Then, an entry about Saint Teresa of Avila, which I skip through in my cave under my grandmother's quilt because I figure I know all I need to know about that particular subject. I am stopped in my tracks though, by one of the photos in the entry about her life and martyrdom in the encyclopedia. In the photograph of the sculpture I see before me depicting this "miracle" at the saint's moment of martyrdom, I recognize the look on the saint's face, and it is the look of orgasmic ecstasy. I can't wait to tell the nuns about the sculpture that the Pope hides away in the Vatican. The famous sculpture is described by all who see it as bordering on "pornography" which is why it is hidden away. I find it interesting that the Vatican is also heading the charge to have Brando's latest films banned everywhere. I was not surprised when Darla told me this latest news on the censorship front. I can't wait to tell her about the story of the Bernini sculpture of the saint I am named after. When I saw the photo, I identified with the cherub angel who penetrates the saint, not the saint. The look of orgasmic ecstasy on the saint's face reminded me of Darla when she comes. Darla would think it was funny, considering what the nuns at school call her. Darla is the reason why I stand up to the nuns. Why I make it my mission to confront them with all that I am learning outside of their Catholic-minded world of confession and punishment and original sin. They hate me. Accuse me of plagiarism every time I pass in a paper. I am fed up. Ready to leave this ironically-called paradise if only I can convince Darla to leave with me.

It is getting harder and harder to see each other at school. I feel like we are being watched all the time. The nuns are going out of their way to keep us apart just like Darla knew they would; they are now trying use the age difference as an excuse. Darla is surprised they took so long to catch on to the fact that, at sixteen, she is two years older than me. But I am sure I'm the only fourteen-year-old kid who went to both high schools with a thick beard growing in. Even the losers who hang out in the parking lot have barely started to shave. The first thing The Doctor did was x-ray me for tumours or growths on my thyroid and in my brain to explain what was going on with my facial hair, but nothing was found. What is happening is different than for other kids, but as far as I'm concerned, it feels natural to want a big dick and a girlfriend. All the boy cousins I used to hang out with wanted the exact same thing. What was the big deal?

We send each other notes through mutual classmates in each other's classes who are sympathetic to our plight and we make a plan to see each other in the baseball dugout after school. It's where all the couples in high school hang out to make out. Before we even start making out, Darla tells me she has something to show me. She pushes her bell-bottom hipster jeans down past her thighs once we are inside the dugout.

She shows me the artwork she did the night before. She has taken a razor blade and cut an undulating snake-like shape into her left thigh. "It's snake magic. For my shaman."

I trace Darla's artfully carved snake from the tip of the tail with the tip of my tongue. Trace my tongue right up to the head of the snake at the top of her thigh. She smiles down at me, daring me to go further. The closer I get with my tongue to her pussy the more she dares me. The cutting will scar, it will be there on her thigh forever. This makes me happy. I lick her pussy for the first time. She tastes delicious, like tart apples. Is this the apple of knowledge Eve urged Adam to bite into? All I know is I am in paradise for real! My tongue flicks over her clit that is engorged and swollen like my dick but much smaller; she pants and cries and pushes my face deeper into her pussy. She wants my tongue inside her. In the name of all the fucking goddesses in the encyclopedia, this is the best! Darla shakes all over, cries out, arches her back and trembles for like what seems forever, then explodes, bucking against my mouth. My lapping tongue is making her come! This is fucking revolutionary!

"Oh my god, that was the best damn orgasm I have ever had," Darla declares, laughing. "Your tongue is a fucking magical snake." She sees me looking at her cutting again. She reads my mind. "I like cutting myself once in a while when the pressure gets too much. I wanted to mark myself for you, you sick fuck." She laughs, pulls me close. "Does my shaman like it?"

"I love it." I tingle all over when she calls me a "sick fuck."

"They call you sick, then I'm sick too," she explains.

We hold each other on the dirt-packed floor of the dugout, looking up at the chain-link fence that surrounds us. I want to be free of chain-link fences, flying up there in the blue sky beyond. Like the first day we met on the beach.

We both come crashing down to earth, back to reality.

"So it will be two years before you're legal? I told my family I had no idea you are only fourteen. You can pass for eighteen easy, I tell them. They believe me, but my family still doesn't want me to have anything to do with you or your family. Something weird is going on with that. My cousins watch me all the time. I can shake them today but it won't be easy to see each other from now on. My old man's orders. I hate him."

WE HAVE TO SNEAK around now, pretend we don't love each other anymore at school. But I still see her on her breaks at work without anyone catching us. We make out under the Overpass, up against the graffiti-covered buttress that holds up part of it, surrounded by broken glass, used condoms, and cigarette butts. We get so carried away making out that she is sometimes late getting back to the bar.

We never see them coming. Caught in the afterglow of our lovemaking, her cousins suddenly tower over us. The full moonlight breaks through the smoke of the Steel Plant behind the three of them, obscuring their angry faces in shadow. Darla jumps up, tries reasoning with them, pleads with them. Two of them grab me, haul me to my feet, the third drives his fist into my guts. Winded, I double over in pain, but it is only the beginning of the punishment they are about to deliver.

"Fucking queer!" they keep yelling at me as their

blows rain down. Darla's screams fade in and out. Their fists beat about my head, they continue until I am a rag doll in their arms. They let me fall, dropping me on the ground, finish off by taking turns kicking me. Satisfied that I am not getting up, they carry Darla off with them.

I hear her yelling back at me, "Birds of a feather! Remember, Terry! Birds of a feather!"

I want to disappear into the earth. I want to die. Rising unsteadily to my feet I stagger home, not ready to face what awaits me: Ma and Dad. The shit will really hit the fan now. My parents are not expecting me. My mother screams at my father to call the cops; Dad curses Darla "the half-breed Artemis slut" when they see the bloody mess.

Soon I can hear the sirens in the distance. I know they are coming here, coming to talk to me, to ask me questions about what happened. I won't tell them anything. When The Doctor arrives after the cops, he pulls rank and takes over. I dread it more when The Doctor sends the cops away. It is the end of me now. I wish the cops would come back and cart me off to juvenile detention, not The Doctor here, who has the power to cart me off to the Butterscotch Palace. Turns out it is Darla they cart off to juvenile detention after they leave my house. My parents blame her for everything. And she will not turn her cousins in to the cops for the beating. The Doctor calls an ambulance and has me taken to the Butterscotch Palace. The nurse wraps up my broken rib, sews and stitches my split lip, and gives me an ice pack for my black eye. And painkillers. My parents won't sign the papers to commit me, so I am sent back home.

The Doctor introduces "Aversion Therapy" as soon I recover from the worst of my wounds. For once he doesn't strap me to the exam table. He lets me sit, facing a projection screen. He tells me he's going to show me some movies. He attaches an electrode to the tip of the middle finger on my right hand. The finger I fuck Darla with. The Doctor must know this. He shows me movies of two beautiful blonde girls in bikinis playing with a Frisbee on the beach. Then the films switch to soft-core lesbian porn. The Doctor flips a switch that delivers a shock to the tip of my finger when it is obvious that I enjoy the porn. The women are beautiful. They kiss, stroke each other's beautiful bodies, hold each other. Watching them you would think they are lovers, tasteful playboy porn that anyone would be turned on by.

He flips the switch a dozen times. I don't let the shocks that jolt through my hand stop me from feeling turned on. I tell him to show me more. I can pass this test, no problem. This enrages The Doctor. I am even more stubborn than Alex in *A Clockwork Orange*. The next time, he straps me back onto the exam table, makes me take my underwear off, he orders the sweet-faced nurse to attach the electrode to my little dick. The nurse looks worried. She doesn't make a move.

The Doctor changes the films we are going to watch. Unlike with Alex in *A Clockwork Orange*, my eyes are not being forced open. I can look away, but I don't. These films are way more explicit. Films of hard-core lesbian porn, the woman fuck each other with huge fake dicks. I am sure he watches these films over and over in the privacy of his office. I get excited, of course. The fake lesbians are hot, and horny, with lots of makeup and long, red fingernails. My little dick hardens. These porn films shock even the sweet-faced nurse. She won't do what he is ordering her to do to me. He tells her again to put a live charge of electricity on my offensive, moist private parts. So he can shock me, make me hate these images, these acts, his version of "Aversion Therapy."

To my utter amazement the nurse grows a backbone, and speaks up. "Doctor, where did these films come from? Why are you showing this hard-core porn to a child? If I attach this electrode to the patient's genitals they will be severely burned. Doctor, what are you thinking?"

The Doctor glares at the nurse in pure disgust. "I am trying to cure this poor monster."

"This child is not a monster, he is a human being. Whatever you do, know that I am a witness."

You could cut the tension in the air with a scalpel.

"Take it away! Just take it away!" The Doctor barks at the nurse who is standing up for me. I don't know if The Doctor means the electrode, or the "monster" that offends him so much, neither of us are sure. The Doctor takes off out of his own office like a bat out of hell. I am sent home.

I can't stand it anymore, and I need to see her. After days of passing notes back and forth using our mutual classmates, she finally agrees to meet me. I am waiting in the dugout, and my heart is pounding out a Led Zeppelin drum riff. I watch her walk towards me through the chain-link fence. Part of me wants to run away. I have been ambushed here before, and have the scars to prove it. I don't see her cousins anywhere. She looks at me like I am a drink, and boy, is she ever thirsty.

Darla passes me her joint through the chain-link fence. I entwine my fingers with hers and squeeze tight. When she touches me everything feels right. Everything else, all the bullshit keeping us apart, is just a nightmare. Looking into each other's eyes is all that matters. Darla looks into my eyes for a long time before she speaks.

"Everyone wants to kill you, for Christ's sake! I hate this place! Some fucking Paradise!" Now the law is involved and everyone is going on about the two-year age difference. The Doctor goes to juvenile court and makes a big stink about Darla taking advantage of a minor, me.

"They're watching me like a hawk."

"Let's go away where they can't keep us apart."

"I can't run away anymore. I'm graduating this year. I'm not going to blow it now." I know she is right but I want things to be different. Running away with me will ruin her plans to get a university scholarship. All Darla ever wanted was to escape from this rough place with dignity. But in that moment I have no dignity; I pout and plead. There is a twelve-foot chain-link fence between us. I am in despair, I want to cry, and rage against the unfairness of it all.

"I just can't see you for awhile. They'll really kill you next time." A tear slides down her cheek as she pulls her hand from mine. "Let's never say goodbye. My grandmother never says goodbye, there is no word for it. It's the Indian way."

We meet up in the dugout and hold each other. Darla kisses me for what seems hours. I want it to be forever. I am in a state of bliss and despair at the same time. Darla is here to say goodbye, the white man's way. I don't want to think about it. My feelings are so overwhelming and conflicting. I can't get enough of her. Maybe I should run away, right now, on my own, without her. We might never make love again. She kisses me passionately, tells me she is going to miss my lips most of all. I am on the verge of tears, but also excited. Those raging teenage hormones are at it again. I want to touch Darla. I skip second base all together, reach for her crotch. She doesn't push my hand away.

"Yes," she purrs in my ear, "I miss your big strong hands. I want your big strong hands to touch me, Pussy Boy."

Darla unzips her acid-washed hipster bell-bottom jeans. That Darla is older and has more experience is intoxicating. She knows what she wants. She doesn't have to tell me twice.

"Touch me now." She pulls me close into her body, and our lips touch. My hand is eager to touch her. She is not wearing any panties! I slide my hand down her trimmed pubes; dip my fuck finger into her. Her lips are wet for me.

"I got wet just walking here. I can't stop thinking about your hands."

My finger strokes her slick, swollen clit. With the tip of her tongue she lets me know she likes this. I love when Darla orders me to put my fingers inside her so I slide one, two, then three fingers inside and start pumping. I see the snake cutting, all healed, not red anymore, just a scar. "More fingers," she demands breathlessly. She wants my whole hand inside her. I am amazed that she can take more of me than I ever dreamed possible. With care, patience and encouraging words from her I slide my whole hand inside. Who needs a big dick when you have a fist at the end of your arm! She is drowning me in her juices. A spot of the dugout's dirt floor is turning to mud under us. I am seriously starting to believe the amount of fluid coming out of her pussy is unstoppable. The air is thick with the scent of her, not the brimstone stench that we were used to around here. Suddenly, and with a tremendous clench, she pushes my hand out of her cunt. She laughs at the wonder of her come hitting my chest. Soaking my working man's shirt, she christens me with her pussy juices. Exhausted she cries out "Pussy Boy!" She collapses back on the bench, pulling me down on top of her for kisses. We kiss for what seems like hours. Darla comes again and again. I'm not even touching her. Then, Darla pushes me up. She opens the buttons of my drenched workingman's shirt. She pulls the shirt off my shoulders down to my waist. I have never let her, or anyone, see my naked chest before. I am nervous, and scared she will think of me differently when she sees these lumps of flesh on my chest that my pals are going gaga over and always trying to grope. I am scared that she will think I should be a girl too, like everybody else. My breasts that I hide from everyone are hers to see, and touch. She licks her lips while looking at them. Then, she cups my breasts in her hands protectively. As usual, Darla knows just what to say; "Ummm, nice man boobs, Pussy Boy. Let's call them 'moobs' shall we? Or would you prefer 'chesticals'?"

We laugh so hard that we piss ourselves, literally.

We are a hot, wet teenage mess. In a dugout, with nowhere to go clean up, we really don't care what we look or smell like when the cops find us walking down the road out of the "lunch bucket" city hours later, after we had been reported missing by both our families. We are trying to get to the Mainland and off this Island Paradise. We want to get away from all the people who judge us, who had the power to keep us apart from each other. There was really nowhere to run, except into the ditch by the side of the road. We let them pick us up, take us to the cop shop, where they separate us. Darla is sent back to juvie hall for trying to run away with me that day. I got off easy. The Doctor failed to have me committed to the Butterscotch Palace because my parents will still not sign the papers. I ask them about it, point blank. I'm tired of all this talk about what to do with me without me being included. I come storming down out of my room while they are talking about it again without me, and demand to know what is going on with the Butterscotch Palace once and for all, are they going to lock me up this time or what?

"That Artemis girl can't get to you anymore where she is, that's enough for us," my mother explained.

"We're not sending you to that place, for now," my old man added, looking at me over the "smoke" he had just rolled. He said this in a serious voice before he licked the glue along the edge of the rolling paper; he finished rolling his cigarette then lit it with his Zippo. "Keep it up though. Just keep it up." He snapped the lighter closed with finality.

THE JUDGE LET HER out of juvie hall after a month and a half. I finally clap eyes on Darla in the auditorium on Spirit Day. She looks over at me without expression. I could be anybody. She doesn't acknowledge me. We are too far apart to speak. I look to her for a sign, something, then realize the nuns are not missing any of this. Nobody is missing any of this. The whole school waits with bated breath to see what will happen. Will we run into each other's arms and be forced apart by the nuns? Both of us carted off, me to the Butterscotch Palace for good, and Darla back to juvenile detention, or worse, back to her father.

Nothing happens. They forget about us. Everybody goes back to Spirit Day.

The school erupts in a display of over-the-top school spirit, cheering and excitement, for the next fifteen minutes. I get my chance when I see her leave the auditorium while it erupts into cheers. I get up and walk out of the auditorium too. I see her duck into the washroom right outside the double doors. I follow her. Unfortunately, one of the crow-like black-garbed nuns follows me.

When Darla sees me come into the washroom after her, she wants to run into my arms, I can feel it. I open my arms. Then, the door opens behind me and the nun catches us together! Right on cue Darla screams, "Stop following me, Terry! Leave me alone! My life is ruined because of you!" Darla runs out of the washroom, brushing past the furious nun, who orders me out of the washroom. Sister escorts me back to the auditorium. Not as noisy now that Spirit Day is winding down and speeches are being made.

Right now my guts are shaking from the impact of Darla's words. My love is unwavering. Darla said those hurtful words for the benefit of the Sister. She didn't mean them. Or did she? My guts heave. What if she does blame me, what if I am stalking her? It is hard not to puke sitting here. I jump up and run to the washroom, I throw up. I am miserable.

Terrified that Darla meant what she screamed at me leaving the washroom, I go to this oak tree we started using as a meeting place. The tree is huge, in the woods and close to the trailer park where she lives. I go to the tree the next night and the next and the night after that. There is a vulva-shaped opening at the base. We leave each other messages in one of my old man's used tobacco cans. Stick the can in the large cunt-shaped hole at the base. I leave a note begging her to see me on the first night, a love poem I stayed up all night writing on the second night, and on the third night both are gone. In their place on the fourth night, I find a note from her, and finally I can breathe. Darla promises to meet me on Saturday night, the next night, after dark. She drew a snake on the other side of the note. I kiss the note with gratitude.

Darla's family spends every Saturday night playing tarbish, a card game everyone on the Island plays. They will most likely be drinking their faces off till they pass out. On this Island Paradise everyone drinks beer like a fish. Nobody will miss her after a few hands at cards and a case or two of beer.

We cannot believe our fucking luck! That very morning, I start bleeding. What the hell is going on with my body? I am not telling The Doctor or anyone. My loins are inflamed, racked with cramp after cramp. I can barely get out of bed. A rolled-up pair of Dad's work socks gives me a basket in my crotch, staunches the blood. In the dank washhouse in the backyard I change into my stash of ripped jeans and a shirt I found last week in the Sally Ann donation box behind the Library. My parents are giving me money for bus fare to the Library now. Dad made good on his threat and sold my dirt bike while I was at school one day.

I wished I could drive the dirt bike off that cliff on the other side of the Island after I saw how Darla acted towards me in the auditorium at school and then in the washroom. And the words she flung at me stung. There could be truth in her words and it scares me. If Darla had not left the note last night, I would have gone out to the trailer park and to hell with the consequences! They could drag me off to the Butterscotch Palace kicking and screaming if it meant I got to see Darla one last time. I needed to hear from her, that it was really over between us.

An early snowfall this afternoon is not going to ruin my night. The moon is full, and the temperature has risen. Here in the woods, under the oak tree, I am surrounded by a light dusting of snow. I am glad I got here before Darla. I spread my grandmother's handmade comforter from off my bed under the sacred oak. Something big is going to happen tonight. I can feel it. I miss talking to her about everything that is going on at home as much as I miss making out with her. I can still feel her lips on mine. Darla comes towards me with a flashlight. She shines the light in my face, obscuring her own from my view. Is she hiding something? Darla can find her way in the woods without a flashlight. I wish she would turn it off, something was not right.

"It's really bright out tonight. Why do you need a flashlight?"

"I didn't want to get lost."

"You could never get lost in these woods, what are

you talking about? What's wrong?"

"Please, Terry, say what you want to say to me. I have to get back before my dog misses me. If that happens my cousins will come looking for me, and if they find us here chatting, we are in deep shit."

"You have a dog?"

"Yes, my old man's new way of keeping track of me. Get me a dog, I can't go anywhere without the beast. My guard dog."

"You were better off in juvie hall. At least you were away from your old man."

"What do you know about it?"

"You're mad at me now? I'm just glad you're not dead. I don't hear from you for weeks. Then you give me the cold shoulder in the auditorium at school on Monday morning. We did talk about suicide the first time we met, practically made a suicide pact. You told me about that cliff on the other side of the Island, remember. I was worried."

"Yes, that was a bad day. We both had fights with our fathers. You told me what you and your old man were fighting about. We never talked about what my old man and I were fighting about."

"I did ask."

"Yes, you did."

"Do you want to tell me now?"

"I want to but I can't. Maybe, I will someday, if

you're still around. Like everyone else in the Pier, you can guess what's going on. It's no secret. But I am dealing with it in my own way. I will hate you, Terry, if you take pity on me. I'm afraid you already do. I don't need your pity. My old man will get his just desserts someday. I'll make sure of that, don't worry."

"But we have to stop seeing each other, is that what you're saying?"

"We have no choice, our families are against us. I don't want it to be my fault that you get locked up in the Butterscotch Palace! Or worse! My old man hates you, Terry. He wants to kill you!"

Why can't we just be in love? Why is our love a crime? It isn't fair. Her old man can do whatever he wants and get away with it.

"Birds of a feather." I take her hand and look into her eyes. I am on the verge of tears. This connection is all I have to hang on to. Darla leans in and kisses me passionately. "Yes, you remember. We are birds of a feather. When I die I will fly like an eagle into the big, beautiful sky, close to the sun. Free at last. Like I said the first day we met."

I put my arms around her. She turns in to me, lets me hold her. After all these weeks, Darla is in my arms where she belongs. I can feel her growing stronger in my arms. I am in paradise again. Darla pushes me down onto my back. We start to make out on my grandmother's comforter. We roll around, laughing like the teenagers we are, teasing each other.

"Oh fuck! I miss my Pussy Boy." Darla declares, kissing me like she can't get enough of me.

I want to die with happiness right then and there. "So does this mean we're back on? We can still see each other?"

"You won't stop until we are, will you. You're not afraid at all, are you?"

"I would take a bullet for you too, you know."

"Don't ever say that! If it comes to that, run! Please, promise me, you will run!" Darla straddles me and pins my arms down above my head. She won't let my arms go until I promise. She is scaring me with her insistence. I know her father is a crazy ex-biker who sells coke and pimps out his own daughter but I can't bring myself to believe he could actually kill people.

"Okay, I promise. I promise to run the other way if that ever happens."

She stares into my eyes intensely, still not letting me go. She squeezes my wrists tighter, not wanting to let me go. She is scaring me. "I like pinning you down like this, Pussy Boy. Reminds me of a fantasy I have about something I want to do to you. You like being in my fantasies don't you, Pussy Boy?"

"Yes," I admit, "I like that a lot."

Darla confesses her fantasy. I get the feeling that from the way she describes her fantasy, she has been nursing this for a while. I have not let her touch me or see my privates yet. For all these months we have been stealing these precious moments together. I am too fucking scared. Will she think I'm a monster too? Reject me? I could not take the chance but I knew it bothered her a lot. The Doctor has me so trained to be ashamed, I feel sick at the thought of being touched by anyone.

"I tie you up to this sacred oak, Pussy Boy. So you can't move, can't go anywhere. I have you all to myself to explore. I touch you anywhere I want and you can't stop me. I find out what you have between your legs. What I find there makes me very happy and amazed. And, really turned on! Trust me, Pussy Boy. I want you!"

I am shaking at the thought of being tied up, and feeling breathless with excitement at the same time. I am overwhelmed by her words. "She wants me!" I want to believe that she really does want me. I want her to be happy with me and I can't make myself believe that she will be. Fear wells up, and suddenly I flash back to The Doctor, and the straps on the exam table in his office. I feel sick, and use all my strength to push her off me. I roll over onto my side, coughing, panting and feeling like I have to get up and run away from her, right now! Or it will all come out, the humiliation, the shame!

"Trust me! I trust you! I would never hurt you, Terry. I just want to touch you without you freaking out, without you pushing me away like this every time."

I feel like I am falling back into a deep hole. The stars above us zoom further away; the oak grows taller in seconds. What is happening to me, am I dying?

"What's the matter? Are you okay, Terry? You're pale as a ghost." She strokes my cheek. "Oh fuck, Terry, you're so cold! Are you in shock? I won't tie you up, don't worry. Tell me what to do! Have I gone too far? Damn, I always go too far! I can't help it! I have so little time. We have so little time."

"I'm bleeding," I blurt out.

"What? Where?" She is not shocked but alarmed, worried.

The darkness is closing in fast and I am falling back. I want to give in to the force pulling me down into the roots of the oak. I want to stay here, look around, explore. Suddenly, I feel a sharp sting across my cheek. I come back to awareness. The full moon fills the sky as bright as day. I feel like a mole, or a snake, coming to the surface. My ears deafened by an explosion of night sounds of the woods. For better or worse, I am back in the land of the living.

"Sorry, Terry. I slapped you across the face. You passed out. No way can we call 911 right now," Darla explains, kissing my stinging cheek, "You're okay. Can I look at what's going on now?" Darla pulls down the pair of my Dad's briefs he thinks he threw out last week. She puts her hand between my legs, and gingerly takes the rolled-up socks from between my loins and finds my "manhood" stained with clots of blood, visible even in the moonlight. Darla is in awe. "Is this your first period? Is this my Pussy Boy's first period?"

Oh, fuck no! The Doctor has been warning me this day would come! Now I know what the fuck is happening. "I thought I was dying," I croak, letting my fear out, finally.

"No, you're not dying, Pussy Boy. Girls bleed every month, too; Nanny calls it "moon time," like the ancestors did. At first I thought you sent away for one of those "sex aids" from the back of *Penthouse*." Darla is talking about the rolled-up socks she holds in her hand. Seeing how much I am hurting, she puts the socks aside and starts massaging my pelvis firmly. The cramps recede under her touch. I calm down and think about what just happened. Where did I go when I passed out? Here under the full moon, tripping on my first period. It was Tiresias' journey too. But I sure as hell don't want to be having a period either! Is this what it was like for double-sexed Tiresias?

"Your first blood. Powerful! Nanny smudges me with sage when I am on my 'moon time', and makes me drink sage tea. Nanny will know which of the sacred medicines to smudge you with. How lucky am I, to be here when you have your first blood, Terry."

Darla's hand massage is helping the cramps go away. I am calm now, and not so upset about bleeding. I was expecting to be rejected because of this bleeding. So afraid this would really be the last time we saw each other.

"All I do is get you in trouble. I'll get you locked up in the Butterscotch Palace. We have to stop."

"What are you talking about? We made a suicide pact the first moment we met on the beach."

"I didn't think it through. You need to stay alive."

"No! I won't, I can't! Not without you. Nobody but you gets that I am really a boy."

"You're a free spirit, Terry, before any sex you are or might become, you have the spirit and gifts of a shaman. Nanny told me you have to live a long life, that 'berdaches' like you must come back to save Mother Earth. My grandmother believes in you, Terry. I can't let you die."

I am devastated, upset by her decision. "But that doesn't mean I don't love you. I am bad news, Terry. Don't love me. It's too dangerous for you. I am crazy about you too, you know. Maybe I should be in the Butterscotch Palace."

"Think they would let us share a room?"

"Yeah, a room next to my mother. She's locked up again."

"I'm sorry, I didn't mean to remind you."

Darla leans in, strokes my bare face, looking me over, taking in every inch of me with her loving eyes, "I really miss your beard. I wish you could grow it back without getting sent to the fucking Butterscotch Palace full time."

"My old man gave me a shaving lesson, though, like I was his son."

"Now, you're bleeding. You are 'berdache', a healer. Where did you go when you passed out?"

"How do you know I went anywhere?"

"Nanny told me that shamans use the 'Tree of Life' to go on journeys to the underground, for knowledge. Here you are, passing out under this oak. You must have gone somewhere."

"I did."

"What was it like?"

"A dark, warm cave. It was scary but I didn't want to leave. I need a guide, though. You could be my guide."

"Nanny could teach you. If our families ever to talk to each other. If they ever let us see each other. You need to meet."

"I don't think that's going to happen anytime soon."

We lie down on the quilted comforter made by my grandmother whom I have never met. We hold each other in the full moonlight that lights up the night sky, our hearts beating together. It is so perfect, this moment. It's like the rest of the fucked-up world faded away. I know that our grandmothers, both hers and mine, are close to us right now, protecting us. Then, the peace is shattered. Darla can't stay away from the trailer park any longer. Her hound dog starts baying for his mistress.

I insist on walking her to the edge of the trailer park, a ten-minute walk through the woods from the oak. On the way, we are aware that sound travels farther in the woods at night. So we don't speak as we walk. An owl hoots overhead. We can't stop to listen to the spooky nighttime woods. Darla's hound dog stops howling. Someone is seeing to the hound and will discover Darla is gone any minute. Or the hound knows Darla is coming, the hound can smell her. When we get to the clearing, she runs ahead to a clothesline near the road where the clearing is more open and windy. There is a quilt hanging on the clothesline, gently lifting into the air and falling back down in the light wind.

The hound dog is tied to one of the clothesline's wooden posts. Darla goes to quiet the dog. He is very happy to see her.

I notice the quilt hanging on the clothesline has

a unique pattern. What could only be the Artemis Clan symbol is very visible in the light of the full moon. I can hardly believe what my eyes are seeing! This comforter has the same pattern as mine! As my grandmother's comforter! The one draped around my shoulders right now. I take that comforter from around my shoulders, and hold it up beside the comforter hanging on the clothesline. They are identical!

Darla sees what I am doing, comparing the two quilts. She signals to not make a sound. She jumps up and touches her fingers to my lips that are about to speak. I have so many questions now. But we are in the middle of her family compound. Her three cousins who beat me up are in a nearby trailer still playing cards. Others are sleeping or passed out in the trailers around us. We might as well be in the middle of a minefield. Not a word can be spoken, too dangerous. Darla leads me quietly back to the overgrown path that no one uses anymore. There are other paths that lead off to who knows where, probably the pot gardens the Clan is rumoured to have planted all over these woods. Darla gives me one more kiss before shoving me back down the way we came.

As I make my way alone, I realize I don't even know when we will see each other again. I didn't care what Darla said about living on after her, I can't imagine living without her. I could steal one of the motorcycles parked in front of her old man's biker bar. What do we have to lose? Absolutely nothing. We are just a couple of "delinquent" kids with no future.

MY MOTHER IS ALREADY asleep, and Dad is working the graveyard shift. In the morning, I try to bring it up, but she won't talk about her childhood. Ma leaves the kitchen and goes into my parents' room, closing the door. Conversation over. I have known for years that her mother died giving birth to her and it's too painful for her to deal with. Darla knows something, probably everything. I ask her why her Nanny's quilt looks just like my grandmother's quilt.

"Find out what your grandmother's name is," suggests Darla, the next time we see each other, this time in the dugout after school. After the three o'clock bell we make sure we are seen leaving separately, to throw off the scent for the nuns. They testified to the judge about Darla's character, and we all know what they think.

We double back, and meet up at the scene of our first lovemaking. We seem to be fooling everybody, me in my tartan skirt and Darla in her very public snubs of me whenever I try to talk to her. Secretly winking at me when the posers she is hanging around with in the other high school's parking lot call me Pussy Boy. We both know it means something different from the way they mean it.

They use it to humiliate me. She uses it to build me up. But only we know that. It's hot too, getting away with it under everyone's noses. We fool everyone.

We are together now in each other's arms in the scarred baseball dugout. I can hardly believe it.

"My grandmother had the same name as my mother's. Marie was named after her. Even worse than being named after Saint Teresa of Avila, both my mother and my grandmother are named after the Virgin Mary."

"Not your grandmother's first name, your grandmother's last name."

"Was it Artemis?"

"Bingo."

"So my grandmother and your grandmother –"

"Are sisters."

"So my mother doesn't want me to find out that we are related?"

"Second cousins."

"So? Second cousins get married around here all the time. What's the big deal?"

"Worse than that, she doesn't want anybody to find out that your mother is just like me, a half-breed. Your mother is afraid of that coming out more than anything."

"My mother is afraid of the truth. I knew something was going on, that night I heard them talking. I knew my mother had secrets."

"That makes you a quarter Native blood," Darla points out.

We don't get what the big deal is about being a "half-breed" to begin with. Darla is upset because she can't claim to be full-blood Native like her beloved Nanny. Not the other way around. Most want to emulate their white heritage. Not the Artemis Clan. I'm upset that I never got to know my Native grandmother. I am determined to find out the truth, even if it hurts. But when I get home there's a note from Ma on the kitchen table. She's gone to bingo with one of my many cousins. Ma has left some cabbage, corned beef and potatoes in a pot in the top shelf of the banked cast-iron stove for me to heat up. The kitchen is toasty warm. Dad is sleeping, of course, in my parents' bedroom off the kitchen, after eating his supper earlier. He leaves for his shift at the steel plant around eleven o'clock. I hope Ma comes home before my old man wakes up.

I put the pot directly on the cast iron stove to heat up the food, a staple on the Island, complete with lumps of steamed flour and water mixed together, called "dumplings," or, as my mother calls them, "dough boys." Pussy Boy eats the "dough boys." I like dipping them in cabbage juice. I do my homework while eating supper. Afterwards, I take a look at the fire in the stove. The wood my mother put in the stove before she left for bingo has burned down. I pull on a pair of gloves and bring in pieces of wood from the woodpile next to the washhouse; fill the woodstove. My father will want a cup of tea before he goes to work.

It's been hours. I am starting to get antsy. At nine o'clock I turn on the TV to watch *All in the Family*. Gloria and The Meathead are my favourite characters. But I can barely follow the show, thinking about what I have to say to my mother. I hope Ma gets home soon. We have lots to talk about before Dad wakes up. I stretch out on my bed, under my new poster of Brando, as "Stanley" in *A Streetcar Named Desire*. I am surprised my father hasn't ripped it off the wall and burned it in the stove. But he hasn't. When I hear my mother come home, I bolt down the rickety stairs and offer to make her a cup of tea.

"You brought in wood and kept the stove burning on your own? My, you are growing up."

"Ma, I start the stove every Sunday morning. So you can sleep in."

"That is you? I thought that was your father."

"Dad showed me how years ago and made me swear not to tell you. You are too much of a worrywart. You'd worry I was going to burn the house down and not be able to sleep in."

"Yes, your father thinks he knows me so well."

Ma wants to know if my homework is done. The usual. I tell her some facts about the origin of "university." Ma shocks me by saying that if I study real hard and graduate, I might be smart enough to go to "university" in a few years. "Your father and I would be so proud."

"What about getting a husband? Like The Doctor says?"

"The Doctor said that? He's putting words into our mouths. Your father and I don't agree with everything that comes out of The Doctor's mouth. Your dad knows you're smart. You can do anything you want, if you put your mind to it."

The fire in the stove is raging, the kitchen is hot and the kettle boils fast. I make the tea. The only tea we have, orange pekoe.

"What about you, Ma? Any luck at bingo?"

"Almost had a full card, but your cousin Agnes beat me to it. That woman has a golden horseshoe up her arse. I'm sure of it. Never going to bingo with her again. And a redhead, like your father, to boot. Redheads have all the luck, they say. She didn't even give me a tip for good luck, kept the whole jackpot to herself!"

This was a mortal sin for bingo-goers, not tipping your bingo buddy.

"Take Dad next time. You know how lucky he is."

"You know what your father says: 'If I didn't have bad luck I wouldn't have any luck at all'."

"He is still working on the skeleton crew at the steel plant, when most of the furnace faces are laid off.

Dad's luck can't be all bad."

"You think working the graveyard shift is lucky? Might as well call it 'the accident waiting to happen' shift. The graveyard shift is a good name for it, too; that's the shift most accidents at the Steel Plant happen on. Most nights I can't sleep when your father's working at that filthy plant. I can't really breathe easy until Dad comes in that door, when he gets home in the morning and starts the fire in the stove. Thanks for getting more wood, dear."

We drink our tea in the cozy, hot kitchen. Ma takes homemade tea biscuits out of the pantry and offers me one. I take it and decide to get to the point. Hoping she will refrain from storming into her bedroom like last time, seeing as Dad is in bed, sleeping before he has to get up for work. This time is sacred to my mother. She would never disturb his sleep just before he leaves for work. Maybe I'll get the answers I need.

"Ma, Dad has more cousins than you can shake a stick at. I need to know more about your side of the family. You must know something about your own mother?"

"That was so long ago, Teresa. Why are you bringing the past up now?"

Ma rocks back and forth, agitated in her rocking chair, one of two things she still has of her mother's. The other thing is the comforter, with the Artemis Clan pattern, on my bed upstairs. She sighs, drinks her tea, and looks off through the window beside her into the darkness of the train yard beyond. She looks old although she is only thirty-five. My father is ten years older than my mother, forty-five.

"Ma, I know you don't like talking about this, but when I was born didn't it come into your head that I would want to know the answers to these questions some day? Like any kid growing up?"

"I have never lied to you," my mother insists. I can see she is close to losing it. She stops rocking and glares at me. "You want the truth? Maybe you can't handle the truth!"

"I know you're a bastard, Ma." I snap back, instantly regretting it. "I heard Dad and you fighting."

"Your father was out of order!"

"So who raped my grandmother? I heard you tell Dad. Who would do that? Are any of his relations still alive? Is *he* still alive?"

"Teresa!"

"My name is Terry! Please stop calling me Teresa. That's not me."

"Believe what you want, I just want the best for you. You are my baby, whatever your name is. Listen to me: stay away from the Artemis family."

"Why does the quilt on my bed have the same pattern as the quilt I saw hanging on the clothesline at the trailer park? Your mother was an Artemis too. Is that why we can't be together? You didn't want me to find out the truth."

"You don't know what it was like back in the day when I was growing up. To be born a bastard was terrible, people whispering behind their hands, judging me. We have that quilt because Nanny Artemis and my mother are sisters. You and Darla are second cousins. Is that what you want to know? Happy now? Nanny Artemis turned her own sister away in her hour of need. You need to stay away from that trailer park. Stay away from that Artemis girl. Besides The Doctor says it's not good for your treatment if you keep seeing each other."

"That's not the only reason we are not allowed to see each other. You kept us apart so I wouldn't find out that I'm part Indian, too. That's just plain racist, Ma."

"You see how they treat Indians around here! Look how those Artemis half-breeds have to live. I am not racist! I am protecting you. Her father is a crook, running a bar that sells drugs and he's white. It's a good thing her father never married my cousin, Darla's mother. She is in and out of the Butterscotch Palace every few months because of that man; your father was talking about her the night you overheard us talking about sending you to the Butterscotch Palace. He doesn't want you to take after her."

"So Dad knows and you are both in cahoots."

"We never dreamed you two would ever meet, much less fall in love."

"We are meant to be together."

"Are you sure about that? I imagine a girl like Darla would be working hard to get out of her situation, if she's as determined to get away from her father as you say she is. A girl that desperate will say anything."

"What are you saying? That she's using me? The Doctor filled me in, said he would commit me if I didn't stop seeing Darla."

"And I'm telling you to do the same! That Artemis girl is using you!"

"You don't know anything, Ma. She loves me! She understands who and what I am. Nobody else does around here. Darla's proud of being a bastard. Proud she carries her grandmother's Indian name, not her white father's white name."

"Proud of being a dirty little half-breed? That's what they call me, your own mother. I want to spare you from that. That's why seeing Darla is bad news. You need to stay away from her. Everybody knows she's been turning tricks since she was twelve."

"She's not bad news for me, Ma. I need her. All of you are wrong about her! She's not some dirty little whore! Her old man makes her do it. We help each other. We want to go to university. Darla's father wants to keep her here on this Island Paradise; you and Dad want to lock me up in the loony bin for refusing to shave off my beard! Everyone goes on and on about what a paradise we live in, but for some of us it's a prison. We have to escape. The Doctor, he told me Darla's father raped her when she was just a little girl." I feel sick to my stomach, just saying it out loud. "And no one did anything! Nobody does anything now! Darla wants to kill herself because of him, and all you can think about is yourself."

"What can we do? Go to the police station and talk to the cops?"

"Yes! Get the charges dropped against Darla, she never laid a hand on me."

Technically it's true, she has not touched me; I touched her.

"Darla says it's useless to tell them about her how her father uses her at the biker bar since they turn a blind eye to all that; they get their cut."

"What?!"

"Darla told me the cops know all about what's going on at the 'Bucket of Blood'. They know all about the drug dealing, and how her old man pimps her out in the back room. She told me her father pays off the cops."

Ma doesn't say a word. She finishes crocheting a square for her afghan, gets up to put a shovelful of coke in the stove. She looks really upset. She doesn't want to believe it. "Your father hates that man, and that bar. If you tell him what you just told me, he will go to the cops. That could just lead to more trouble. Better just leave things."

I concede. I see the danger to my old man if he takes on Darla's father. A beating in a dark alley late at night would be the least of it. I am torn between protecting my father and getting help for Darla.

DARLA HAS BEEN avoiding me for weeks, playing it very cool in the hallways at school. I thought we were back together. But something happened, because Darla is different. Really different. It was like those promises we made to each other under the oak tree had never happened. Last week when she was out in the parking lot with her cousins, it hit me like a bolt of lightning! Darla is knocked up! She is a few months along, enough to show even from where I was standing. She has a baby bump. I get her alone in the girls' washroom later that day, just before the three o'clock bell. Darla tries to leave. I come between Darla and the door. I'm not going to let her leave without agreeing to see me, she owes me that much.

"We have to talk."

"Your father can still have me arrested, remember? Let me go, Terry."

"I talked to my mom. I know your grandmother and

my grandmother were sisters. My Ma says Nanny turned her back on her own sister, that's why my mother doesn't want to have anything to do with the Artemis Clan. But I talked to my Ma, told her what you told me about all the things that go on at the 'Bucket of Blood'. She talked my old man into dropping the charges against you. But they're scared, too."

"They should be. You and your parents shouldn't get involved. I am going straight to hell just like all the nuns say. Terry, you let me down. I never want to see that look on your face again."

I am horrified. She saw the look that came over my face when I realized she is pregnant. I knew it couldn't be mine, but at the same time, I wish I had knocked her up. I want the father to be me. I try to explain the mixed emotions I am feeling in that moment. "I'm in shock. Could you not have sent me a message at the oak tree? I will be the baby's father. I've thought about it, I will take care of both you and the baby."

Darla laughs, cynical in the midst of her despair. "You're fifteen, not thirty, remember? I wish you were the father, Terry. I really do. But we both know that was just a game we played. You're living in a fool's paradise if you believe in all the games I play. Paradise is for suckers. I can't fight this battle for the right to exist on my own terms anymore. I need to leave, Terry!"

I'm afraid she means the Island, or worse, the known world. Is she going to go flying off that cliff on the other side of the Island without me? I can't let her do that.

"Take me with you!"

"No, Terry. We talked about this. You don't really want to leave, you just want the world to be a different place. Maybe it will be, if you stay. You're going to do great things, I know it. So you can't leave."

"Meet me. Let me give you a reason to stay."

"If we get caught, my father will kill us. I am warning you, Pussy Boy!"

"Meet me at the sacred oak. We'll be safe there."

"I can't, Terry. I can't put you in danger. I'll never forget the sacred oak tree and what we did there for as long as I live." Darla looks at me and I can see the desire in her eyes. I tingle all over and press my advantage.

"Miss my hands?" I reach out and touch her baby bump. I cannot help it. I reach out to caress her protectively, possessively. I want both Darla and the baby she is carrying to be mine. Did I spill my imaginary seed into her womb? Could it have been me? I want to believe it.

"Of course I miss your hands; your strong, manly, but gentle hands." She places her hands over mine on her belly. "Now the baby will miss them too. Please, don't make this any harder than it is."

"Listen, don't give up. We'll come up with a plan together. Meet me at the sacred oak tree tonight. Just see me, please."

I pull Darla into my arms and kiss her. For this family we could have. Darla agrees to meet me later that night under the sacred oak. We leave the washroom separately, careful not to get caught together by the nuns.

All I could think about the rest of the day was kissing and touching Darla. Now that she is here, I feel shy. "See that comet? That comet up there in the dark hasn't been seen for over 150,000 years. I read somewhere that Pink Floyd's new album, *Dark Side of the Moon*, is inspired by this comet. On the news they say it's the Comet of the Century."

"You really think that comet up there can change anything?"

"We can hope it brings about change in the world, can't we?"

"You're such an idealist, Terry. A real, sweet Pussy Boy. Don't turn out mean, like most men."

"Someday people like us will not have to sneak around to see each other like this."

"People like us? Native people you mean? Half-breeds like us? Queers like us?"

Darla leans in and starts kissing me. We start making out.

"Can I still touch you when you're knocked up?"

"Oh, yes. My pleasure won't hurt the baby. I have sex with you in my dreams all the time, and wake up feeling really horny. Nanny says it's a sign from the 'dream lodge'." She lowers her voice to tell me the rest. "Nanny's a medicine woman, a midwife. I was scared to tell you. She could go to jail for being a healer, too. No one can know that she uses the sacred medicines since the whites banned them years ago. Instead, they use drugs and shame women who feel pleasure when they give birth. Nanny will take care of me, don't worry."

"What does Nanny think of your dreams about me?" I dream about her too and feel the same heat when I wake up. Then reality sets in and I want to die.

"That we are meant to be together, right now. Nanny believes this baby is special. She follows the comet too. That's why I'm here now."

I am in awe of her words. "Nanny is very wise. I think she's right about the Dream Lodge. I dreamt about you, on my birthday."

"I could feel you fucking my pussy, Pussy Boy. We don't have to be in the same room to fuck each other. I love that. I refused to work at the bar that day. I told my father I was sick so I could stay home dreaming about you on your birthday."

"You dreamt about me all day? I like that you defied

your old man, and I thought about you all day, too."

She meows in my ear and pulls me on top of her. We make out, knowing we are together on borrowed time. The enormity of our situation betrays us. We pull apart, aware of how much trouble we are in if we get caught. We are panting, almost crying. We hold each other tight and weep in each other's arms.

We are both victims. Despite the two-year age difference between us, we are both still just kids. But we are treated differently because of it. Darla is called a predator and I am her victim. Nothing could be further from the truth. We are soul mates torn apart by powers we are helpless to fight, much less change.

"This is real life, Terry. We have no power and we can never be a family. It's just not possible to have dreams anymore. The nuns are throwing me out of school, disqualifying me for all the scholarships I applied for."

I am totally helpless in the face of her despair. "You know what they'll do to me, and I know what they'll do to you. Staying apart is the only answer that makes sense, for now. Can't you see that, Pussy Boy?"

I could see she was right. If only there was some way.

"But you know where I am, right?"

"With Nanny, in the trailer park?"

"Yes, that's where I'll be, if my father doesn't send me away."

93

"Away? Why? Where would he send you?"

"To the Big Smoke. His sister, my Aunt Kitty, lives there."

"Why would he send you away?"

"It won't come to that." She doesn't want to talk about it. "He won't send me away, don't worry."

"But what if he does? We have to run away. That's what we have to do."

"How? We have nowhere to run and I need Nanny's help. The cops will pick us up before we even make it to the Mainland."

"This isn't fair!"

"Why would he send you away? So no one will find out he's the father?"

Darla shoves me away, jumps to her feet, she looks down at me with shame, dread, and then rage. "Fuck you, Terry. Don't go there!"

"Fuck me? What about him? I hate that he gets away with this, but we can't be together. We can't even go to the cops."

"I told you, they are paid to ignore what goes on at the bar. You are so fucking naïve, Terry. You have no idea what goes on in the minds of adult men. That's why I love it that you're both. Or neither. Or...you know what I mean."

"I've got The Doctor to deal with. Believe me, I

know. The Doctor can mutilate me at will, if he wants. My own father can have me committed! Nothing you tell me will surprise me."

"He has a gun. He tapes it up under the bar. I think about taking that gun and blowing his brains out with it all the time. Who could blame me? I'd be doing the world a favour."

"No! Don't do it that way. They'll send you to prison."

"Not if I make it to that cliff I told you about, on the other side of the Island, before they catch me."

"What if we got a lawyer to help us?"

"Lawyers want money. Do you have money to pay a lawyer?"

"No, of course not."

"We just have to come to our senses, for now. We can't see other. I'll think of you the whole time we're apart. But Terry, we need to be cool. My father is really mad."

"Maybe we should set him up."

"We have to be smart about this, Terry. It's not just you and me now. No. We play it cool, for now."

"We can still meet up here after the baby's born, can't we? I'll be able to see the baby, right?"

"Terry, don't get your hopes up. I can't give my father any excuse to send me and the baby away, remember."

"Not even once in a while?"

"That might not be until my father is either dead or in jail. But he pays off the cops, so that will never happen. I wish my cousins would tune him up, instead of you. They like his money more than him. If a wedge could be driven between my father and my cousins, they might come around and help us. Maybe I will tell them you're their cousin, too."

"Why is this happening? If I wasn't queer, this wouldn't be happening."

"It's not your fault. None of this is your fault. I'm queer too! I am sick of being told what to do all the time, believe me, but I have to think of the baby. He will kill the baby if we are not careful. That's what I can't stop thinking about. I have to protect the baby. Remember that first time? I begged you to knock me up? I never let boys fuck me the way you fuck me, Pussy Boy. That first time was so fucking hot. I wanted your baby in that moment more than I wanted to kill myself. I'll never forget you roaring up out of nowhere, on the edge of that cliff above me, riding your dirt bike. I knew then we were meant to be together. I wanted you, Pussy Boy. You give me reason to live, to survive. You and me, and the baby makes three. Nanny believes this happened to bind us three together. We both believe this is your baby, not his. Never his!"

We hold each other and look up at the comet. We watch the tail streak across the night sky, all colours like a rainbow. "Our baby will change the world." Darla kisses my ear. "Now, I want to touch you. I want to touch my Pussy Boy. I won't be able to touch my Pussy Boy for a long time."

A shiver goes down my back, I want to go there. I want to give her what she wants. I whisper in her ear, "So what are you waiting for? Touch me."

We make out like the teenagers we are, lips swallowing lips, tongues sliding, hips grinding, hands stroking each other. Then, Darla straddles me; she rubs herself against the bulge at the crotch of my dungarees. She gazes down at me, takes my hands and places them on her baby bump. She rides me with bliss on her face. Darla rides me with her hands over mine, still on her belly. I hold her like this while she bucks against my "manhood." The comet still streaks across the heavens just beyond her shoulder, as she comes in deep, long shuddering waves. When she comes, the look on her face reminds me of Saint Teresa, the one I was named after, on the moment of her "martyrdom."

"I saved all that pussy juice up for you, Pussy Boy, to seal the deal," she says, laughing. My dungarees are soaked through with her juices, a giant wet spot, on my crotch. "No matter what people say, remember: this baby is *our* baby."

"Next year on my birthday, when I turn sixteen,

we'll be together," I vow.

Darla agrees. The baby, her and I will be together again, as a family. It was just another one of those ironical situations, like "rough paradise," that keeps us both at the mercy of others more powerful than us. Until then.

We hold on to each other for dear life. Listen to the mournful sounds of the woods at night. Listen to each other breathing. Our hearts beat in unison, as one heart. We gaze up at the full moon, drifting in and out of shared visions and dreams. All of them will have to be put on hold till the rest of the world catches up with us. My body hums with conflicting feelings, intense sadness to intense joy, from one moment to the next and back. I had read many love poems at the Library, and many times they said that this is what love does; it fucks you up. But you really don't get it from reading the poems, until you fall in love yourself. Does it fuck everybody up this good? This bad? To be content just to have Darla in my arms, here and now, is all I want. But we are marked. We don't have much time. I realize I need to stay in the moment. Right now is all we have.

"I need to know my Pussy Boy will keep his promises."

"I keep my promises."

"Are you sure you know what you're promising me?"

"To tell everybody I'm the baby's father, no matter what anyone else says to the contrary. Don't let anyone know the truth, especially the baby. Don't ever let our baby find out who their real father is."

"Yes. Perfect. That's exactly what I need you to promise."

"I promise on my life."

"I love you, Pussy Boy. You must never forget that either."

All my walls crumble when she touches me now, her sounds of delight, telling me how much she loves her Pussy Boy over and over. I go back and forth, from where I am in utter bliss with Darla under the oak, to a cold, sterile room in my head. In the middle is the exam table where I am tortured. I manage to drive The Doctor away, lock the room shut from the outside, and stay in my body when she strokes me, licks me, penetrates me with her fingers. Her passionate kisses excite me. She is the best kisser, and I could kiss her forever. She tells me I am beautiful, with awe in her voice when she sees my privates for the first time, and I believe her. I go deep into my body for the first time with another human being. I buck at the end of her fist, cry out in my cracked voice. I have my first shameless orgasm. I give myself to her. I give my virgin "mangina" for the first time, to my first love, the love of my life.

Without warning a voice in the woods calls Darla's

name. Spooks her. We pull apart and hastily pull ourselves together. Darla panics. She is afraid one of her three cousins is coming down the path, looking for her. We can't be caught together. She has to get back to the trailer park. They notice she is not there. They must have checked in on Nanny.

I insist on walking her back. One of her cousins is calling for her. They are looking for her. We can hear them calling her name close to us. We get to edge where the three trailers take up the clearing in the woods. Yellow light spills out of the windows of the trailer where Darla lives into the darkness surrounding the trailers. Patsy Cline belts out "I'm Crazy for Loving You" on the eight-track.

Her cousins don't see us but I won't let Darla go just yet. I kneel before her in the moonlight and kiss her belly, kiss our baby. She strokes the back of my head. "Always remember the baby." She looks into my eyes so intently, her hazel eyes unforgettable. I take Darla in my arms to kiss her goodbye. Just as our lips touch for maybe the last time, all hell breaks loose.

"Get away from our cousin, you freak."

"Yeah, you fucking queer! Stay away from our cousin!"

"Or we'll sic the dogs on you this time!"

One of them holds the ax from the woodpile in his hands. It's like a scene from a horror movie.

"Terry is one of us!" She yells in their angry faces, ready to inflect more pain on me. She fearlessly snatches the ax out of her cousin's hands. "I'm putting this ax back in the woodpile where it belongs. Axes are for chopping wood, not people. Call off the dogs, for fuck's sake, guys! Terry's mother and my mother are first cousins. Terry and I are second cousins. We are all cousins here."

The cousins, my cousins, are still skeptical.

"But it's still queer!" one cousin exclaims.

"I am too, you dumb ass! You heard them call me a 'lezzy' for years! Well, it's true!"

"But you're one of us!"

"Yes, and so is Terry! You know who you should really be pissed at? My old man for tricking you boners into beating the shit out of one of our own! You should all be ashamed of yourselves!" Darla is really laying it on thick, and it's working. The three of them do look pretty ashamed.

I LEFT THEM YELLING at each other about going to confront Darla's old man, for making fools of them. I had to get away before he showed up. I am, by proxy, now the "father" of an unborn baby. Darla is going to be the mother of her own sister or brother. Everybody will know the true origins of this child. I had promised to tell a lie to protect the child and I had to make everyone believe it. There was no doubt in my mind that her old man would kill Darla if she ever told him she made me the baby's "father" tonight. If she ever does say anything about our pact under the comet, our baby is dead. If that happens, Darla is dead too. Unless I get my hands on a gun and kill him first myself.

I trudge back home under a full moon. The comet filled me with these crazy ideas. I am desperate and I walk home with murder on my mind. When I get home, Ma is sitting in her rocking chair, with her coat still on, quietly crying. She jumps up and hugs me when I come in the door. "So glad you're home, dear. Something terrible has happened, I heard about it at bingo and I can't stop crying, it's so terrible."

"What is it, Ma?" I look into her beautiful face, so like Darla's. She could be her mother too, and her tear-soaked face is softened by a love I have not seen for a while. I take her hand and hold it. It is trembling with emotion. She hasn't put her house slippers on yet either. Bingo was over hours ago. How long has she been sitting here in our cold kitchen, crying?

Ma wipes her eyes, and steels herself to tell me what happened. "Your cousin Agnes' boy Danny was killed in a hit-and-run coming home from school today. He is only two years younger than you, Teresa. Witnesses said it was a drunk driver. They said the car was weaving all over the road like a drunken sailor."

"Oh no! Danny's dead!"

"The other kids said Danny was walking by the side of the road, he bent over to tie a shoelace and the driver swerved right into him, took his head clean off his shoulders. Then kept right on going! Oh my God! Awful those kids had to see such a terrible sight! They'll be having nightmares for years! Poor Agnes! To know your child died in such a horrible way! I was worried about you! Where have you been?"

Do I tell her where I've been? Tell Ma what I've done? Tell her the promise I've made to Darla? Which would make her a grandmother?

"I had to see Darla."

"She's in trouble, I know. That Artemis girl is the talk of the bingo hall too, in case you don't know it. Why are you putting yourself in harm's way? Have you got a death wish or something?"

"I love her, Ma! We will be a family some day! Darla, the baby and I, just the three of us, as soon as I turn sixteen."

"Don't talk so crazy, Teresa! You don't have anything to do with that baby! Everyone knows it's his! Her own father's! I don't know my own neighbourhood anymore, since that bar opened up. Don't know my own mind since you turned twelve and started growing a beard. I thought

I was helping you but I guess I just made things worse! I thought I was protecting you from the Artemis Clan. I don't believe the Butterscotch Palace can fix this anymore, you're too far gone."

"I'm in love. Why is that crazy? Why is that a crime?"

"You are infatuated, that's all, it will pass. It's not good for your treatment. That's what The Doctor told your father and me."

"The Doctor don't know dick."

"Teresa!"

Dad strolls into the room from their bedroom just off the kitchen. He is up, getting ready for work.

"What's all the waterworks for, Ma? I can hear you two balling your heads off out here, and you let the stove go out. Did someone die? Did I miss something?"

Ma tells Dad about Danny. He takes the bad news in stoically. He sits down at the kitchen table to roll his smokes before he goes to work. Cousin Danny was his spitting image, a redhead like him. I liked Danny because, before I discovered the encyclopedia, Danny had the best comic collection in the neighbourhood. We used to trade comics back before puberty hit and I got kicked out of Paradise for being me.

Dad will be a pallbearer at Danny's funeral. A few cousins died of drink, while others died stone-cold sober in fatal accidents at the dangerous, man-eating Steel Plant. I even have a cousin who died in a gas explosion in a coalmine that goes deep under the ocean on the other side of the Island. My old man is a pallbearer at all the cousins' funerals, every time.

"Drunk drivers should be strung up and publicly horse-whipped," my old man quips, off the cuff, as usual.

Dad strikes the business end of a matchstick against the iron stove and the match flares up. He pulls the match up to light his rolled smoke but is interrupted by a sudden pounding on our front door. Dad curses quietly under his breath and makes a move to open the door.

No one with any sense would be pounding on our door at this time of night unless it was really fucking serious. Someone must be dead, another accident at the Steel Plant.

"Who's pounding on my door this time of night?" My father looks at us both, as if we have x-ray vision and can see through the door. One very angry man was calling my father out.

"Who's out there?" Dad doesn't want to answer but they just keep pounding.

Dad pulls on his frayed, faded blue working man's shirt and goes over to the door. He gestures at us both to go upstairs. He will handle this. Ma doesn't have to be told twice. She grabs my hand and pulls me up the stairs after her. My cat, Pussy, is spooked too. She tears up the stairs ahead of us.

"Calm down! I'll open the door!" We hear Dad yell at whoever is out there.

The pounding halts. We hear my father open the door a moment later.

"What the hell is going on? Has someone been killed at the Plant?"

"Someone will get killed tonight, all right, if your freak of a kid doesn't stay away from my daughter!" Darla's father! Holy fucking hell! The cousins must have confronted him! Now he is here on our porch!

"Well, if it isn't the big shot who whores his own daughter out!"

Darla's old man looms in the doorway; he is a big man, built like a biker gone to seed, but he is not as big as my old man, who is built like a steelworker, a "furnace face" who does a lot of the heavy lifting with his shovel. The degenerate, drug-addled bar owner tries to punch my father in the face. Darla's old man had a few beers, and a probably few toots of coke, before showing up here. Dad has about three inches on him. Dad is stone-cold sober as well. He takes his furnace duties seriously. Other men's lives are in his hands.

"You come around here and threaten my kid again and I'll kick your ass into next week! Get your junkie, son-of-a-bitch ass out of here!" Dad turns the intruder around in the doorway, and pushes him out onto the porch. Once he is out in the yard, the coast is clear and Ma and I run down to watch what happens next from the porch. Dad hustles the drunken intruder back out on the street, with his punching arm twisted up behind his back.

Dad lets Darla's old man loose, and he turns and tries to clobber my father with his fists. Dad has no choice but to punch him in the gut, hard. The bastard goes down like a sack of shit. I cheer my father on for Darla's sake.

"Don't sink to that devil's level!" My mother warns.

My old man watches a winded, drunk, coked-up, angry ex-biker get his bearings and half-crawl, half-run off, holding his guts, into the night. "I'll kill you and your freaky kid. Don't go anywhere! I'm getting my gun and coming back to shoot you and that freak dead! All of you are dead!"

"Bring it on, you piece of shit! I'll be waiting for you!"

"Me, too," Ma pipes up, shaking her fist. "We'll all be waiting for you! Our whole family will be waiting for you!"

I can hardly believe what I am hearing. My mother and father are sticking up for me! My father turns away from the monster he managed to scare off. Dad steps back up on the porch, with disappointment on his face.

"Now look what you've brought on your family, a degenerate like that, threatening my kid! Listen to us when we tell you to stay away from that Artemis girl. She is bad news."

"You can't keep us apart anymore. Ma told me everything! I know we are second cousins. I know Ma's half Indian. Nobody cares anymore. Now, there's no excuse to keep us apart!"

"Oh, is that so? You're not sixteen yet, so yes, I can keep you apart! If you don't stop seeing that girl I will commit you to that Butterscotch Palace so fast it will make your head spin! You might never get out! So you want to be a degenerate like her and that father of hers? I am trying to save you here, can't you see that?"

"It's not easy being a kid like me, Dad. The Doctor calls me a monster and maybe he's right, I bring trouble right to your door. I know you call me a 'heathen', and maybe that's what I am, but why can't you accept me? You created this monster. You created my body. You are both a part of me! You need to stop trying to change me. 'Teresa' never was. My name is Terry and always has been. You named me, deal with it!"

I run out back to the washhouse and dig out this ugly housedress they make me wear. I took it off before I went to meet Darla at the oak tonight. Ma is rocking back and forth slowly in my grandmother's chair. Dad is sitting at the kitchen table rolling his smokes for work. They look up when I come in the back door. I bunch the housedress up in my hands and shove it in the stove, pile sticks of wood over it. Make it sure it burns.

I turn back and look from Ma to Dad.

"Darla is my girlfriend. We love each other, like girlfriend and boyfriend. She has to be welcome here. She has to feel safe here. Ma, do you want us hanging out in dugouts and in the woods? Where anything can happen? We have no place to see each other! It's not fair!"

Ma and Dad look at each other, they look at me. Ma sighs. Dad goes back to rolling smokes. "Get out of those filthy rags. At least let your mother wash them for you."

I start to take my shirt off gingerly. They see the ragged undershirt I am wearing underneath. "Throw that t-shirt back in the rag pile under the kitchen sink where you found it. I'll give you a new one."

I can't believe they are not freaking out. Dad has second thoughts, though, when I take off the dungarees and he sees the briefs, stuffed with a pair of his thrown-away work socks. "Oh, that's it! We can't let it go this far, Ma. This is moving much too fast."

"Dad, you need to catch up. Or, slide back off. We had a terrible tragedy here in our neighbourhood today.

Danny is dead, just walking home from school. Death can strike anytime, anywhere these days, even here. We're not going to have any more fights over this. You know it's the worst place. Besides, that Doctor gives me the creeps."

Ma turns to me. "Go to our room and get Terry clean clothes."

Dad says nothing, gets up, and heads to the bedroom. He comes back out with a worn t-shirt and a working man's shirt, gives them to me. I'm stunned, silent. I never thought this day would come.

"Ma's right. Life is too short. I worry about you, Terry. I don't want you to get treated badly, out there in the big, bad world. I thought I was doing the right thing, making you wear that dress, and shaving your beard. But you're right. You are from both of us, you are our kid. Whatever you are, remember, you are still our kid. We have to protect you."

"Not from Darla, Dad. From everyone else. From the nuns. And, from The Doctor. From the cops."

"You have a blind spot where that Darla is concerned. Love *is* blind, they say. It must be true. Terry, you are not old enough to keep seeing Darla. She is older than you, and also more experienced. The law is the law. That is not going to change."

"I'll wait. She'll wait until I turn sixteen, then we can do what we want."

"Well, let's see how she fares over the next year. If she sticks it out till you're old enough to make your own decisions, then I hope all this is not for nothing. What you're putting yourself through. What you're putting this family through. We just had the devil himself show up at our door. The villagers with pitchforks can't be far behind."

"Once it gets out that we are letting you be yourself, the way you want to be in this world, there might be hell to pay. Not for just you, Terry," my mother points out.

My dad says the last thing he wants to admit. "You might have to move to the Big Smoke, if you want to get help. See a doctor who really knows more about this condition you were born with, if you want to love someone and be happy."

The next thing my father does really amazes me. He takes the committal papers for the Butterscotch Palace out of the drawer in the kitchen table, walks over to the stove, lifts the round lid off the top and shoves the papers into the flames. This makes me happy.

"Don't be so happy. Being a man's no piece of cake, being a man's more than just a change of clothes. You have to get a job, support yourself. You bring home the bacon, now, is that what you want? If I teach you like a son, I teach you to stand on your own two feet, and I'll be tougher on a son than on a daughter."

"Maybe you could be both, tough and tender?" I suggest.

I go upstairs and put on the pants and t-shirt that Dad just gave me. This one is tighter across what Darla has dubbed my "moobs," pushes them closer into my body. The newer t-shirt binds them down better. I pull on the "pièce de résistance," the blue work shirt that my father wore.

I go back downstairs, feeling like I am really home, at last, in my own skin. I answer my parents.

"This is what I want, yes."

"What about school? You'll have to go back to your old high school; the nuns are never going let you go to the girls' school now."

"They already kicked me out."

"I'd give it a week or so before you see that Artemis girl again. Give that crazy father of hers time to calm down."

"I thought you said I couldn't see Darla?"

"I said according to the law."

"You're not worried he's coming back with a gun? He has one, you know, taped up under the bar. Darla told me."

"He's all talk. He won't put that bar on the line for the likes of us. He can't be that stupid," my dad insists. I hope he's right. "He can't go around shooting people, don't worry."

I have no idea what Darla is going through right then, though. I start to worry. What was he doing here in the first place? He knows we are seeing each other. What could he be doing to Darla right now? I hope she and the baby are safe with Nanny Artemis. She won't let anything happen to them.

"Please tell the rest of the family to stop calling me Teresa." I want to be able to dress like this in front of all my family and be accepted.

"OK, we'll tell everyone to call you Terry, not Teresa anymore." My old man concedes, after looking to Ma for her two cents. She nods her agreement.

"Actually, I want to legally change my name to Terence. As soon as possible." There I had said it. Let the chips fall where they may. Had I gone too far? Only time would tell, I guess. The Doctor doesn't show up with the white-clad, muscle-bound orderlies in tow the next day, so I figure I am safe.

I did not see or hear from Darla anytime the next week. I am alarmed when she doesn't show up at the parking lot after school. We are going to the same school again. The nuns kicked her out, too. I leave messages in the tobacco tin at the sacred oak tree's vulva mailbox. Still no messages from her. No sign that she got mine. Something is not right.

On the verge of disguising my voice and calling

the cops to report her missing, Darla finally shows up at the parking lot with her cousins. They never let her out of their sight. I am shocked. She looks so different. Her bump is gone. Darla is not pregnant anymore. I feel sick. The cousins warn me away with a look. We can see each other from afar, but we can't speak. We can't even acknowledge each other. I can see that Darla really is different; she looks at me with such pain and fear. What did her father do to her? I refuse to give up. I continue to leave her messages in our secret mailbox. Once in a while, the messages are gone. No message from her is ever in its place. I feel like I have been kicked out of Paradise, my fool's paradise. In the midst of my misery, I am afraid that Darla's beautiful spirit has been crushed. She looks like she doesn't want to live anymore.

I cry about the baby that will never be, our baby. I can't take it anymore. I sneak out of the house and make my way to the back alley behind the "Bucket of Blood."

She has her joint lit before she sees me in the shadows and walks over to me like it's the most natural thing in the world. She pushes me up against the brick wall. "What took you so fucking long?"

"I'm going crazy with worry. I had to see you. What happened? Where's our baby?"

"My father took me to a doctor, forced me to get rid of her, what do you think?"

I want to puke right there and then. Does this man have no shame? No humanity?

"I think I'm going to be sick."

"If my father comes out that door and catches you here, you will be dead, never mind sick. He has a gun under the bar, remember."

"He won't get away with it."

"I am his property. And this property is condemned."

"Don't talk like that. Have I brought all this on?"

"Don't flatter yourself. I brought all this on by being born with a vagina. A pussy rented out by my own father. I wish I could get to that gun, but he is always standing at the bar."

"Please, don't kill him. Let's just hitch a ride to the Big Smoke. Tomorrow. My parents might even take you in, hide you."

"That's the first place he'll look, Terry! I know he'll find us wherever we go." Then she looks at me with those almond-shaped eyes, devours me. "You look different, more confident. Did you stop seeing that quack? What happened to you?"

"My old man and I don't fight anymore. I wear whatever I like. I told my parents that I'm changing my name to Terence. They didn't call The Doctor, or anything."

"That's good to know." She seems relieved. "You

need your parents on your side. I'm glad at least one of us has parents who look out for them. My Nanny looked after me after my father brought me home from that doctor of his. I almost died. Nanny took care of me with her sacred medicines. But now I wish I had died. I let him take our baby! I'm so sorry!" We stand in the shadows of the alley holding each other tight, tears streaming down our faces over the loss of our baby.

"I didn't even get to hear her cry," Darla keeps saying over and over.

I would have had a baby girl to take care of, if it wasn't for him. He's a monster!

The ancient metal back door swings open on its rusty hinges.

"Well, isn't this a sweet reunion?"

Darla's father sounds fake. Nobody knows his real name and everybody calls him by his old biker name, Snake. Is it any wonder I haven't called the man by name till now? Is this the "snake medicine" I am supposed to take on? Is this the snake Tiresias struck on the ground with his shaman's staff?

"Well now, I hate to cut this short, but you two are breaking the law right now. I can call the cops. Like that!" He snaps his fingers. At least he is not pointing a gun at me.

"Just five minutes alone, please, Daddy?"

"Maybe I'll go do that, right now!"

The way she calls him "Daddy" makes me want to puke.

"I'll make it up to you later, please? Five minutes?"

He stares at his own daughter with such shameless lust, right in front of me. I am shocked. He relents at her words. I don't want to know how she will make it up to him for granting her the privilege of speaking to me for five minutes, but it's probably something awful. I try not to go there, not to think about it. Not to talk about it. I'm on the edge of madness.

"What will you have to do to make it up to him?"

"Don't ask. You really don't want to know."

"There's my answer. Fuck! I want to kill him myself."

Darla shoves me back into the shadows with her hand over my mouth. "Don't worry, Daddy, I'll take care of this Pussy Boy." She says it the way her cousins do, she says it back over her shoulder to her father still standing in the doorway, not yet ready to retreat back into the bar.

"That freak doesn't come back. You remember what I told you. Get whatever it is to wise up, and stop bothering you. My daughter is meant for better things."

Finally, he goes back inside, leaves us alone. Miraculously alone. In a filthy back alley. We can hear Janis Joplin singing "Summertime" from inside.

"What's he talking about?"

"Never mind. That's just some talk. He says he's sending me to work in a club up in the Big Smoke. I think he wants to get rid of me, somehow. I know too much, Terry."

"My old man can protect you," I offer, not even knowing if it is true. I'm grasping at straws.

"No. I won't let your parents get back on his radar any more than they already are." Darla won't listen to any of my pleas to leave with me, right there and then. She shuts me up by making out with me up against the brick wall, puts my hand between her legs. Her pussy is wet. Very wet. She swings me around till her back is up against the brick wall. She spreads her legs, and I fall to my knees. I push her tight miniskirt up above her hips, I pull aside her soaked panties. I sniff her pussy. The scent of her excited pussy excites me. I explore her labia with my tongue until I find her clit. I lick her for all I'm worth. She shudders against my mouth, pulling my hair as she cries out. We've been here at it a lot more than five minutes.

Next thing I know, she pushes me away.

"Fuck off now! If you don't want to feel the business end of his gun in the back of your head before you die, fuck off now!"

Darla is talking strangely, like she is talking for an audience, a special audience. Of one. I know now this is all for show, that she let him watch. I stumble to my feet, run away and try not to look back. I knew I'd see something between them, something he wanted me to see. He knew I wouldn't be able to resist.

After that, I don't see Darla anywhere. She doesn't come back to school. Darla is gone now. Nobody will say where.

One day, her father sends me a message. My mother's screams of terror bring the old man and me running. The head of Darla's hound dog is on the porch, right in front of our door. A terrible sight. It remains fresh in my mind. How many times had Darla told me how jealous of her dog her father was? Now, I am terrified for Darla. Has her father killed her, too? I hope and pray he has indeed spirited her off to the Big Smoke. At least she's far away from him. All I know is Darla is nowhere to be found on this island. Not on this so-called "paradise." I can only find her in the pages of my "rough paradise."

The Doctor found out my parents let me stop wearing dresses. Let me wear the clothes I want to wear. He hit the roof when I showed up as "Terence" for my last appointment, wearing new hipster jeans and a paisley-patterned men's shirt. Ma scraped the money together to buy me this outfit at the Sally Ann's second-hand store, for my birthday. She donated back the dress that she originally bought me.

It was a gamble walking into his office, deep in the Butterscotch Palace, as myself. I tossed and turned the night before, but I know that as long as my parents burned the commitment papers I am safe. He can't lock me up without their consent. I say my piece; leave the fear of ever being locked up in the Butterscotch Palace behind. I tell him I will spill the beans about his "special treatments." I am blowing the lid off this "Aversion Therapy" scam; I, too, have done my research. If he tries to commit me, which would mean getting the law involved, if he tries to go over my parents' heads, I tell him he'll have a tell-all battle on his hands. Best of all, I tell The Doctor, to his face, if he ever gets his shit together he should try and help people like me, not treat us like monsters. It feels good to get that off my chest.

The Doctor takes a long look at me over his glasses. "I was only trying to help you, Teresa-Terence-Terry. Help you make a choice. This was all a part of the treatment plan I had mapped out for you after I researched the latest treatment for your particular kind of Gender Identity Disorder. But now you've committed yourself to this path."

"I haven't had any complaints yet, Doc." I interrupt his bullshit. "You were my biggest challenge. Just you. Nobody else, including my parents, had a problem with me, until you stuck your nose in. You turned my parents against me, and threatened me with mutilation. You raped me. But, they're on my side now, and for that I have nobody to thank but myself. I believe in myself. I know who I am. I always did. That's the one thing you couldn't destroy with "aversion" therapy" or your "special treatments."

After I leave the Butterscotch Palace, the nurse runs after me waving a brown envelope. I take it from her, curious. She found a doctor in the Big Smoke who treats people like me, a doctor who does "sex reassignment surgery," but to be a man, not a woman. I look at the contents. They include newspaper clippings of others like me, who were coming forward. I am blown away! There *are* others like me out there! I knew it!

"Thank you!" The nurse is saving my life again! She wishes me luck and gives me a hug. Along with the new clothes, I have a new beard growing in.

I still endure the terror of not knowing what happened to Darla. Even if I did get to the Big Smoke, where would I begin to start looking? Would my seer powers lead me to her? I am out of my mind with worry. I am starting to believe she is dead. I wonder if she jumped off that cliff on the other side of the Island without me. I hitch a ride to the cliff and look over the edge. It is a straight drop right down into the crashing ocean waves. I want to follow her off that cliff, but I remember her words. I remember I promised I would go on without her, no matter what.

"Don't let the bastards destroy you!" Darla implored. "Or another Tiresias. Don't let them kill a future shaman. The world needs more healers like you, Terry. Besides, I promised Nanny I would keep you alive."

Even as I pause on the edge, Darla's words come to me just in time. "You need to stay alive to tell the story of those of us who couldn't make it."

One day, I am at the oak, crying for her. I find myself running through the woods, in the direction of the trailer park. I must see Nanny Artemis, my great aunt. She must tell me where Darla is. Nanny is hanging clothes up on the clothesline when I show up unannounced. The Artemis Clan quilt is hanging on the line, again.

"Where is Darla, Nanny?"

Nanny says not a word. The grey-haired grandmother, my kin, just stares at me, entranced.

"It's Terry, your sister Marie's grandkid, the 'berdache'. You called me that, Darla told me."

"My granddaughter is missing. Only you can find her."

"So, she's alive?"

"Alive or dead, only you can find her, with your seeing powers. Dream on it."

"Will you teach me how?"

"There's not enough time for everything you will

need to know for your healing journey. You will meet other teachers. They will come to you, in many forms, human and animal. But you have to leave this island." Nanny is just as heartbroken as I am. She doesn't know where Darla is either.

Other times, all i want to do is get to the Big Smoke and search for her. Find my Darla. I go through periods when I refuse to believe she is dead. What was the point? I have no one to talk to.

Sometimes, I wish I could go back to a time before puberty. A time before blood, before hair, before the shame that began when I was fourteen. My father just wanted to keep me safe, out of trouble. He was just doing what The Doctor told him was right. He figured it out. Came around and was sorry for what he did. Darla's father was a monster. He put her to work in the bar when she was only sixteen. Nobody said a word. Nobody helped. They took their cut and looked the other way. Last I heard, Darla's father got caught selling massive amounts of coke out of the bar and his bribes and connections weren't enough. He deserved what he got. He is under lock and key and away from young girls.

At fourteen, I met Darla and believed I would never be alone again. Memories of our time together flood my mind, and my heart sings again. Aches again. Weeps again. I miss her so much and have been alone ever since she disappeared. Ma and Dad don't know what to do. But, at least they try.

As soon as I turn sixteen next week, I've got my ride over the Overpass. Dad and I have spent the last six months getting a second-hand motorcycle ready for the trip. I am going to ride down, up, and around the asphalt traffic cloverleaf on a real motorcycle. Say goodbye to the Overpass, and Steel Plant-dominated skyline, and the prison created where the sky meets the water, and the threat of the Butterscotch Palace. Hopefully, for good. I'm going to make it across the Causeway, off the Island and onto the Mainland on my two-wheeled freedom, on my way to the bright, pretty, pink neon lights of the Big Smoke.

Where my life awaits. Where I might find Darla. Where I might fall in love, again.

Acknowledgements

I would like to acknowledge the support of the Toronto Arts Council, my beloved dog Daisy for 16 beautiful years together, and finally I would like to acknowledge the love of my friends and supporters from all over the world.

Other Quattro Fiction